Table of (

Copyright

1

***

"Aunt Lisbeth! Aunt Lisbeth!"

Jacob, my godson, flung himself into my arms and I groaned as his four-year-old weight slammed against me.

"You're getting heavy, bub," I said, pushing his blonde hair out of his eyes.

Jacob's eyes twinkled and he burst out laughing. "You're getting heavy," he repeated.

I rolled my eyes. "Alex, your son is at it again!"

Alex, my best friend, next door neighbor, and Jacob's mother, burst out laughing. She twined her black hair into a messy bun before giving Jacob a mock-stern glance.

"Sweetie, you know you're never supposed to say something to a woman about her weight," Alex teased.

Jacob laughed again, his cheeks flushed with the effort of it all. After a second, I joined in. I was sure that he didn't understand what the "grown-ups" were talking about, but that didn't matter – he just liked being in on the fun.

Alex yawned. "My shift last night was killer," she said, rubbing her eyes. As usual, the huge rock of a diamond on her left ring finger caught my eye. "I swear those college kids…they're like animals. They don't know when to quit!"

I snickered. "That's what you get," I teased, sliding Jacob off my lap and getting to my feet. "I couldn't ever be around jerks like that. It would drive me mental."

Alex nodded. "I mean, the money is good…sometimes. But let's just say I appreciate only having to work three days a week." She smiled and yawned, suddenly looking very smug.

Immediately, I dropped my glance to her midsection. It was just as toned as ever.

"Don't tell me you're already pregnant," I said, too quietly for Jacob to hear.

Alex blushed. "Not yet," she said. "But…we *are* thinking about trying."

I laughed. It had almost been a year since Alex had gone through what I liked to call 'The Romance of the Century.' A gorgeous, wealthy lawyer had strolled into the bar where she worked and swept her off her feet. They'd fallen in love, despite Alex's hesitations, and they'd been married for about six months. I'd never seen a couple happier, or more in love, than Alex and Billy.

"Good luck," I said. I laughed. "Better you than me."

Alex laughed shortly. "Yeah," she said. "Not gonna lie, pregnancy isn't very much fun." She gave Jacob an adoring glance. "But it's all worth it," she added.

I nodded, biting my lip.

Alex's face fell. "Oh, Elisabeth," she said. "I'm sorry." She flushed. "I shouldn't have said anything."

I waved my hand in the air and wrinkled my nose. "Don't worry about it," I said. "I was always on the fence when it came to having kids, you know that."

Alex nodded. She lowered her voice so Jacob wouldn't hear. "Just think of being shackled to that asshole," she said quietly.

I shuddered. "Yeah," I said softly. "At least I don't have to co-parent with a cheating liar."

Alex opened her mouth and just as she was about to speak, the front door opened and slammed shut. I stood up, wiping my palms on my thighs.

"That's weird," Alex said. "Billy normally doesn't come home until—"

Just then, Alex's husband Billy stormed into the room. He was a handsome man – a little too much of an ex-frat kid for my taste – but with his deeply tanned skin and dark blonde hair, he looked every inch the Successful Southern Lawyer. Normally, Billy was friendly and easy-going. But today, his lips were twisted in a scowl and there were noticeable dark circles under his blue eyes.

"Fuckin' hell," Billy muttered, taking off his jacket and throwing it on the couch. "I need a drink."

"Jacob, sweetie, time for you nap," I said, reaching down for Jacob. He ran over to Billy and gave him a quick hug.

"Daddy is going to spend some time with Mommy, okay?" Billy asked, ruffling Jacob's hair.

Jacob smiled happily. He held out his arms to me and I scooped him up, holding him high in the air and zooming him through the air.

"Airplane!" Jacob shrieked with laughter. "Airplane!"

For once, Billy didn't look overjoyed at Jacob's antics. He jerked his head to the side, indicating that I was to take him to bed right away. I rolled my eyes. *What's eating him*, I thought as I started carrying Jacob out of the living room. *He's usually so tolerant!*

Jacob was practically falling asleep in my arms as I carried him down the hall. His lips were sticky with spit and I gently set him down in his new "big kid" bed.

"There you go, partner," I said, pulling the blanket over Jacob's legs. "Take a snooze. Mom and Dad will be there when you wake up."

Jacob yawned, unable to keep his big blue eyes open a mere second longer. I watched him fondly for a second. While I didn't exactly regret not having kids of my own, sometimes I wondered what it would have been like. Jacob was a great kid – Alex was lucky that he'd always been so easy to take care of. Knowing my luck, I probably would have wound up with a perpetually colicky, bratty child. Still, I wondered what it would have been like. When I was growing up, I'd always wanted to be a mother.

I'd been an only child – a lot of the time, my friends who had siblings told me I was lucky – but sometimes, I felt like I'd missed out. Now I was resigned to the fact that it wasn't going to happen.

Oh, well. At least I still had my pottery.

When I got back to the living room, Alex handed me a glass of wine. Her brow was creased.

"He's on the warpath," Alex whispered under her breath. I raised my eyebrows. Just as I was about to ask what she meant, Billy stormed into the room. He'd changed out of his three-piece suit into some dark jeans and a polo shirt, and he was gripping a crystal tumbler filled to the brim with whiskey. His face was tense and angry, and he kept pacing around the living room in small circles.

"What happened?" I sipped my wine and lowered myself down onto the couch.

"Fuckin' crazy divorce at the office," Billy said. He raked a hand through his thick blonde hair.

"It's like, really bad," Alex clarified. "You want me to tell her?"

Billy looked tired and drawn. "I shouldn't really be talkin' about this," he said, his thick Georgia drawl underlining each word. "But I know you won't say nothin', will you?"

I shook my head and shared a mischievous look with Alex.

"Of course not," I said primly. "You just know how much I love to gossip."

Billy rolled his eyes. "Well, this here is the damn divorce of the century," he said. "The husband's a real brooder, you know, he probably read too much damn poetry when he was growing up."

"That doesn't sound so bad," I said, picturing Mr. Rochester in my head. "He's intense. So, what?"

Billy exhaled forcefully, then poured half of the whiskey down his throat. "His wife, she's fuckin' nuts," he said. "She's like, gonna boil the bunny. Know what I mean?"

I laughed. "Yeah, okay, that sounds pretty crazy," I said. "But what's so bad about it?" I wrinkled my nose. "Divorces are *always* ugly," I added. "And I speak from experience."

An image of my ex-husband, Richard, popped into my head and I had to resist the urge to growl and throw my glass of wine at the wall. Richard had been my first – my first *everything*. We'd been high-school sweethearts, ever since I was fifteen and he was seventeen. Everyone had called us the "living proof that opposites attract."

Just goes to show that you shouldn't ever believe those old adages.

"Hey, Elisabeth," Alex said, waving her hand in front of my face. "You okay?"

I nodded. "Yeah," I said. If it had just been Alex and me, I might've said something about Richard. But even though I liked Billy and felt comfortable around him, I wasn't necessarily comfortable talking about my failed marriage.

"I think I'm gonna get going," I said, getting to my feet and stretching. "I'll give you guys some privacy."

"Oh, you should stay for dinner," Alex said. "I'm making this new recipe – a chicken enchilada skillet."

I forced a laugh. "No thanks," I said. "You guys enjoy."

Alex gave me a hug and walked me to the door. Just as I was about to leave, she eyed me.

"Hey, everything okay?"

I nodded. "I'm fine," I said. "I just..." I trailed off, biting my lip. "I just feel like such a fuck-up sometimes." I looked to the ceiling so I wouldn't start to cry.

Alex hugged me again. "You are not a fuck-up," she said firmly. "You have me, and a godson who adores you."

"I know," I said. I gave her a small smile. "And trust me, I'd go totally nuts without both of you. You keep me sane."

Alex grinned. "We try," she said. "I'll see you later, okay?"

"Yup, see you," I said, opening the door and letting myself out of Alex's condo.

It was a two-minute walk to my own front door, but it felt like it took forever. I was biting the inside of my mouth, trying not to cry as the bright Georgia sunshine streamed into my eyes. *Fucking bastard*, I thought, balling my hands into fists. *You ruined my life*.

Richard and I had gotten married young – three years into our relationship, when I was eighteen and he was twenty. He joined the Navy almost immediately, and after that, we moved all around the country while he did…whatever it was that men in the Navy did on bases in seemingly every city with a port. For a long time, we'd been in San Diego, which I'd loved. But one night, Richard had come home and told me that we were moving.

To Georgia.

"I hate the south," I'd said, putting my foot down firmly on the floor. "Why the hell did you agree to this without asking me?"

Richard had sighed. "Baby, it wasn't up to me, you know that," he'd replied. "They make all the decisions for us. That's what I get for signing my life over to Uncle Sam."

I'd frowned. "Still, they normally give you a little notice," I'd said slowly. "It's weird that they didn't mention it before now."

Richard had shrugged. "Oh well," he'd said. "Don't worry about it. Savannah's not like the rest of the south – they've got all those artsy-fartsy people that you'll just love."

I'd rolled my eyes. In retrospect, I should've known that something fishy was going on. While Richard wasn't a champion communicator, he'd usually tell me little day-to-day things. But all that had tapered off recently, and I'd finally begun to wonder why.

In the end, we were only in Savannah for a month when I found out. Richard was having an affair with the wife of his corporal, who also conveniently happened to be his best friend. I came home early from a pottery retreat and found her blowing him in our bed. Richard had begged forgiveness, and at first I wasn't exactly opposed to the idea. After all, we'd been together nearly ten years at that point. I was still young – I didn't want to be a twenty-eight-year-old divorcee. But when Richard told me that the affair had been going on for years, I was devastated. I couldn't believe that he'd lied to my face for so long…not to mention put me at risk for disease, as he and Trish hadn't used protection.

The divorce was quick and dirty. I was able to prove adultery with the help of cell phone records, and Richard was ordered to pay me fifteen hundred dollars per month. It wasn't a lot, but it did help me out. I'd never gotten anything higher than a high-school diploma, and I only occasionally worked, selling pottery and teaching small classes when I got too restless. Now, Richard lived in Japan. He and Trish were married, and I'd heard through the grapevine that they had four kids.

That had been over five years ago. Sometimes, it still felt like yesterday.

2

***

The next day, I was mostly over it. After five years, I honestly didn't think of Richard very often...but sometimes, I just couldn't help it. I was feeling a little embarrassed at how quickly I'd darted off from Alex and Billy's place, so I called Alex and asked if she wanted to come over.

Ten minutes later, Alex was at the door with a bottle of wine and some delicious-looking cupcakes, covered in luscious icing.

"This looks great," I said. "I'm not even hungry but I could eat the whole box."

Alex laughed. "They're from that new bakery downtown," she said. She rolled her eyes. "Billy thinks it's too chichi, but a client brought him these and let's just say he didn't say no."

I laughed. "How's Jacob doing?"

Alex wrinkled her nose. "I think he likes pre-school so far," she said. "It's only a half-day program, and they do a lot of fun activities. Although he brought home arithmetic homework yesterday, can you believe that?"

I burst out laughing. "You're kidding! He's four!"

Alex shook her head. "Billy about shit a brick," she said. "He almost wanted to pull him out and put him in a different program, but I told Billy that stability is the most important thing, especially since Jacob is just starting. I wouldn't want him thinking that whining for one afternoon is enough to change the world."

I shook my head. "Still, though. Homework!"

Alex laughed. "Yeah," she said. "I was expecting like, finger-painting and making little necklaces out of macaroni. But I guess things have changed since I was a kid."

"Don't I know it," I said darkly. I took the bottle of wine from Alex and carried it into the kitchen. After hunting for a corkscrew, I poured two generous glasses and handed one to Alex.

"To pre-school," Alex said. We clinked. She took a long sip. "I can't believe how fast Jacob is growing up," she added. "It seems like just last week that it he was a baby."

I laughed. "I know," I said. I'd known Alex ever since she had been pregnant – I'd moved in next door shortly after my divorce was finalized. We'd become instant friends, despite the massive differences between us.

"Hey," I said, leaning back on the couch and sipping my wine. "When are you guys gonna get a new place, anyway?"

Alex rolled her eyes. "Ask the King about that," she joked. "Billy is *so* picky! He just had this tiny little apartment before he met me, so I didn't think he cared that much. But he's turning out to be like Goldilocks. Every house is too small, or too old, or too big, or too *something*!"

I laughed. "I bet," I said dryly. "I hope you guys don't move too far away. I'm definitely going to miss being right next door. Besides, my new neighbors will probably be assholes."

"I hope not," Alex said. "We want to keep Jacob in the same school district, this one is the best in Savannah."

"I'm sensing there's a hidden 'but' there," I said.

Alex shrugged and looked guilty. "Billy sometimes talks about moving to Atlanta," she said. "He wants to start his own firm, and move away from civil cases. But I don't know how serious he is."

"What about you?"

Alex's cheeks flushed pink and she shook her head. "No idea," she said. "If we have another baby, Billy doesn't want me to work outside of the house. And I wouldn't mind that," she said. "But I'd feel guilty about starting now. Jacob will be in kindergarten next year, so it's not really like I'd have a lot to do during the day."

"Wow," I said. "I can't imagine that."

"I know, you've been sitting for us for years." Alex smiled. "You're a real lifesaver, Elisabeth."

"Remind me to call and ask you to repeat that sometime," I said dryly. "Like, whenever I need a little pick-me-up."

"Speaking of that," Alex said, refilling her glass and then handing me the bottle. I laughed – I was already starting to feel a little tipsy.

"I'm glad you came over," I said. "I feel like we don't get a lot of girls' time anymore."

"I know, I feel so terrible about that," Alex replied. "But I have to admit, I do have kind of an ulterior motive."

"Oh yeah?" I took a long drink, savoring the juicy flavor as it burst in my mouth. "Lemme guess – you're going on a second honeymoon, and you want me to watch Jacob?"

"Nothing like that," Alex said.

"Good," I said. I laughed. "Because I thought I was going nuts before. Babysitting for a few hours is a lot different than making sure that your house is kid-proof for a week!"

Alex laughed. "No," she said. She bit her lip, looking pale and furtive. "Promise you won't say anything about this?"

I narrowed my eyes. "What's going on?"

"Well," Alex straightened up, tossing her black hair over her shoulder in a businesslike way. "I did a little…research last night, on that client of Billy's."

"The nightmare divorce guy?"

Alex nodded. "He's a billionaire," she said,

raising her eyebrows. "He owns this consulting firm that works freight and logistics."

"I don't even know what that means."

"Neither do I." Alex laughed. "But he's got like, tons of money. The only reason Billy agreed to take his case is because this is going to be his highest-paying client."

I nodded. "That makes sense. But I don't really get why you're telling me this."

Alex flushed. "He has two little girls, twins, they're five years old." She fumbled with her phone before pulling up a photo and passing the screen to me. Two adorable pale little girls with dark hair and dark eyes glowered at the camera. They were wearing matching pink frilly dresses, and looked like they wanted to murder whomever had dressed them.

"Cute," I said. "So, what's the deal?"

Alex looked pained. "Well, he's probably going to lose his kids, even though his wife is a total piece of trash. She doesn't parent them – Damien is the only one who cares, and he's terrified of losing custody."

"I know the courts usually favor the wife, but if she's so awful, why does he think he'll lose them?"

Alex shrugged. "She was a stay at home mom, or at least, that's what she called herself. But Billy told me she'd hire babysitters almost every day, then go out and party or shop for hours. Or lock herself in her bedroom with her *boyfriend* and snort coke all day."

"That's terrible," I said. "Those poor kids. No wonder they look so pissed."

Alex nodded. "Yeah," she said. "Billy is really concerned. He doesn't want to lose this case. Apparently, Damien has a real hell of a temper."

I bit my lip. "And his wife cheated on him?"

"With the VP of his firm!"

"No!"

"Yes," Alex said, nodding.

An intense dislike of this woman – who I'd never even seen, much less spoken to – bubbled up inside of me and I downed the rest of my wine, reaching for the bottle.

"Cheaters are vile," I said. I shuddered. "What a bitch."

Alex nodded. "Yeah," she said. "I thought you'd say that."

"Anyway, why tell me all of this?"

Alex shifted and looked uncomfortable. "I have an idea," she said. "It came to me last night, when I was up and I couldn't sleep."

"What is it?"

"It's silly."

I rolled my eyes. "No, this is silly," I said. "Come on, Alex. You know I hate being kept in the dark."

"Come over for dinner tonight and I'll tell you and Billy," Alex said slowly. "Because if he doesn't approve, there's no way this is going to work."

Narrowing my lids at her, I reached for a cupcake and ate the whole thing in one bite. The sugar was so intense that it almost burned my tongue, but the treat was delicious and I closed my eyes.

"Seriously, tell me – why can't I get a job drinking wine and eating cupcakes all day?"

Alex laughed. "I have no idea," she said. "But when you find one, give me a referral."

We laughed together, but I wasn't really paying attention. Damien, Billy's rich client, was at the forefront of my mind. I pictured him as puffy and covered with a bad orange spray tan. *He's probably a workaholic*, I thought. *And she cheated because he was never around, or something like that. He probably wears one of those tacky gold chains around his neck and never takes off his wraparound sunglasses.*

When Alex and I polished off the wine, she left to go start dinner and I lay down for a nap. By the time I got up, it was six-thirty. I changed into a cotton sundress, pulled my light brown hair back in a fishtail braid, and grabbed a fresh loaf of bread from the deli along with a few fancy cheeses.

I couldn't deny that I was extremely interested in Alex's "idea." But I didn't understand – why was she involving me? Did she just need someone to confer with?

Either way, I knew I'd find out soon.

When I knocked on the front door, Jacob ran outside and hugged me around the legs.

"Aunt Lisbeth! Aunt Lisbeth!"

I laughed and reached down to ruffle his blonde hair. "Have a good day at school, kiddo?"

"No," Jacob said sourly. He stuck his lower lip far into the air. "It was bad."

"He's lying," Alex called from inside. "He had a great day."

"I did not," Jacob said firmly.

I laughed. "I get it," I said. "Come on, let's go inside and help your mom."

Alex was standing at the stove in a cocktail dress and an apron. I did a double-take when I realized she was wearing makeup.

"You look great," I said, setting the bread and Brie down on the table. "You sure I'm not interrupting date night?"

Alex laughed. "No," she said. "I just...well," she turned, tugging down the front of her dress and exposing her slim cleavage. "I want to give Billy something nice to look at."

I raised my eyebrow. "And...why is that?" I walked over to the fridge and helped myself to a beer. "Are you going to give him some bad news?"

Alex chuckled. "I hope not," she said.

Twenty minutes later, Alex, Billy, and I were sitting at the table. Jacob was playing in his room, and Alex had cued soft music to play in the background.

"How was your day?" Alex asked Billy. She reached across the table and took his hand. "I love that tie on you," she said, reaching out and stroking it.

Billy narrowed his eyes. "Okay, sweetie," he said. "You can cut the crap now. What's going on?"

Alex flushed. "I don't know what you mean," she said innocently.

Billy and I burst out laughing.

"Come on, babe," Billy drawled. "You haven't worn makeup since the wedding, and I don't think you've *ever* made marinara sauce from scratch."

Alex bit her lip. "Well, the truth is…I do have an idea," she said softly.

Here we go, I thought. My palms began to sweat with anticipation and I wiped them on my dress.

"Oh yeah?" Billy raised an eyebrow. "Lay it on me, babe."

"Don't you think Elisabeth looks respectable?"

"What?"

Alex turned to me. "Elisabeth, you look really respectable," she said. "Like a nice, well-adjusted young woman."

"What the hell is going on," I asked slowly. "What are you getting at?"

Alex giggled and took a sip of her wine. "What if Elisabeth pretends to be Damien's new girlfriend?"

"What?" Billy and I spoke at the same time. Our jaws dropped in unison.

"Alex, why the hell would I do that?" I asked.

"Because you look like a stable influence on Damien's life," Alex said meaningfully. "You could be, oh, I don't know. A role model for the kids! So, the court doesn't think Damien would be a bad father. It would help, Billy, I just know it would!"

Billy snorted. "Absolutely not," he said firmly.

"Why?" Alex turned to me. "Elisabeth, come on! You could do it! You could help this guy keep his kids!"

Billy clenched his jaw. "Darlin' forgive me, but that is the stupidest thing you've ever said," he said. He shook his head angrily. "That is about fifteen different kinds of illegal, not to mention completely amoral!"

"I don't think it's that bad," Alex said. "It's not like we're hurting anyone!"

"You'd be hurting the legal process," Billy snapped. "I could lose my license! I could go to prison, Alex. That would be *fraud*!" He shook his head. "I can't believe you! If anyone finds out that I tried to sway a judge, my name would be mud around here."

Alex narrowed her eyes. "Fine," she said stiffly. "Forget it. It was a dumb idea anyway."

"Yes," Billy said. He sighed. "It was. And it's not happening." He eyed me. "Elisabeth, don't you go gettin' any ideas now, you hear me?"

I nodded. "Of course," I said. "You don't have anything to worry about."

Billy's eyes flashed with annoyance. "Good," he said. "Because that's the last time this will be discussed." He turned to Alex. "You hear me?"

"Of course," Alex said sweetly. "You're right – it's a bad idea, and I never should have gone along with it."

But when Billy excused himself to get a refill of beer, Alex turned to me and winked. My stomach sank. *She can't possibly think this is a good idea*, I thought.

Still, I couldn't deny that I found the prospect intriguing.

3

***

When I got home from Alex and Billy's, I poured myself a glass of wine and sat down with my computer. Not that I intended to do anything rash, but I was so curious about Damien now. What did he look like? What kind of guy was he?

Probably not my type, I thought as I typed his name into Google. The aforementioned image of the puffy, smug CEO was firmly launched in my brain. But when I turned to "Images," my jaw dropped.

Damien Edwards was no fat CEO with a bad spray tan. He didn't even *look* like a CEO. He looked like a rock star, or maybe some trendy owner of a bar. He was tall and lean, but on the slenderer side. His long dark hair flopped in his eyes. And his eyes...his eyes were the deepest pools of black I'd ever seen. They were shiny, intense hunks of coal that seemed to penetrate my soul through the computer screen.

I shivered. This was certainly not the man I was expecting.

Searching further down the page, I found a photo that made my stomach twist and shrivel. Damien was wearing casual clothes – dark jeans and a black t-shirt – and he had his arm around a gorgeous woman with caramel-colored hair. She was dressed in expensive but similarly casual clothing, and she had a smug grin on her lips – which I could tell were almost certainly enhanced with collagen.

The caption read: "Family Man and Business Triumph – Damien Edwards on the Balance Between Work and Play."

I clicked on the picture and it took me to the business section of *The Savannah Gazette*. The article had been published only two years ago. As I read it, a bad taste seeped into my mouth.

"At thirty-seven years old, Damien Edwards is only just beginning to dominate the world of freight and logistics consulting. But with an MBA from Harvard and a beautiful wife by his side, he says he's more than ready for the challenge.

Unlike many businessmen, Edwards says the key to success isn't just hard work and intelligence. He shows a softer side, speaking about his wife, Candace Edwards.

'Candace is my world,' Edwards says, affectionately squeezing his wife. 'Without her, I'd be nothing.'

Edwards is also an active father. He says he enjoys the role. 'My girls are three right now – twins,' Edwards explains. 'It's my goal to raise my girls, Arabella and Annaliese, the exact same way my father raised me.'

Edwards' father, the late Thomas Edwards IV, founded Global Visions when he was a young man out of college. After his death, the twenty-five-year-old Damien Edwards took over the company, and began a new era of consulting success.

'Dad raised me to be humble, to be proud of myself – but not to rest on my achievements,' Edwards says, his eyes gleaming with humility. 'I aim to be more like my father every day.'

I couldn't read anymore. I closed my laptop and closed my eyes, tilting my head back. Maybe it was just the wine, but something deep inside of me was suddenly very curious about Damien Edwards. And it wasn't just because he was wealthy...although that didn't hurt. For one, he'd looked completely different than what I'd expected. And he was obviously smart – he wasn't just some bloated kid who'd taken over his father's business. If anything, based on the coverage, he'd only made Global Visions more profitable and famous.

It wasn't particularly late, but I crawled out of my sundress and into bed, pulling the covers over my body and nestling into the pillows. After five years of sleeping on my own, I'd developed a curious habit of occupying the middle of the bed. But now, I wondered what it would be like to share my bed with someone like Damien...if only for a night. My skin grew hot and flushed as I imagined how it would feel to be in his strong arms. He obviously took care of himself, but he wasn't too muscular – I liked that. I'd always preferred skinny, artsy guys anyway. Oddly, Richard and I had been total opposites. Back when I'd first found out about his affair, I'd blamed that.

Now, however, I knew that it was because we were completely incompatible. We always had been. I'd just been too young and stupid to see it.

When I finally drifted off to sleep, I dreamt that Damien and I were making love. We were in my pottery studio, and he was holding me against the wall, making me squirm and moan and writhe in ways I'd never felt before. I woke up hot and flushed and damp between the legs, my bedroom filled with the scent of my arousal.

--

In the morning, I got dressed and went over to Alex's. She was cheerfully bustling around the kitchen, cleaning up after breakfast.

"I want to do it," I said flatly, before I'd even sat down.

Alex narrowed her eyes. "What?"

"I want to do it," I repeated. "I mean, I want to help Damien."

Alex shook her head. "Oh, no," she said. "You heard Billy last night. And he was completely right, may I add. This would be terrible – if a judge found out, he could be banned from practicing the law."

I bit my lip. "Well, I don't want to pose as his girlfriend or fiancée or anything like that...but I do want to help."

Alex looked nervous. "Billy is going to be so pissed," she said. She sighed, sitting down and the table and shaking her head. "I mean, you know, I'm all for it. But he'd be so angry with me if he found out."

"I don't want to lie," I said quickly. "But what if we just met for drinks or something? What if we just had a date and got to know each other? There's no harm in that, is there?"

Alex bit her lip. She still looked skeptical. "I don't know," she said.

"Come on," I begged. "It was your idea, and I know you still think it's a great one."

"It isn't that," Alex said. "But you know I would never do anything jeopardize Billy's career."

"Oh, I know," I said. "That's why I want you to ask him again."

Alex burst out laughing. "No way," she said. She adopted a stern look. "Now lookie here," she said, mocking Billy's thick Georgian twang. "I ain't gonna be hearin' no more about that!"

I snickered. "Come on," I said. "He's like butter in your hands. You can totally do this."

Alex looked unconvinced.

I sighed. "I mean, if it makes you totally uncomfortable, then don't do it," I said quickly. "But I really think it's time for me to start moving on. I mean, casually – I don't really want anything serious, at least not right now."

Alex cocked her head to the side. "What makes you say that?"

I blushed. "I looked him up last night, online," I said. "And this sounds really shallow, but he's so gorgeous. It made me feel alive again, you know? Like it made me feel that I still have blood in my veins."

Alex nodded. "Of course you do," she said. "But why now?"

I shrugged. "Alex, I'm thirty-three," I said. "I'm not getting any younger. I know I'm not going to have the same kind of luck as you – you know, the whole fairy-tale thing – but I don't really want to be alone for the rest of my life."

"You've dated," Alex pointed out. "I mean, a few times."

I wrinkled my nose. "Yeah, with stoners from the pottery shop who can't even remember my name." I rolled my eyes. "I went on like, three days with Jeremy before he even realized who I was!"

Alex giggled. "That's because you're an *artist*," she said, rolling her eyes. "You're always going to have to deal with people who are a little off."

I nodded. "I know. That's why I want to meet Damien. He really looks like he has his shit together."

"He does, I think," Alex said.

"Not to mention, we've already got something in common," I said dryly. "A cheating, lying former spouse who didn't give a flying fuck about ruining our lives."

Alex nodded. "Hey, I'm sorry if this dragged up any bad memories for you," she said. "I hope it hasn't made you think about Richard too much."

I rolled my eyes. "Thinking about Richard at all is thinking about him too much," I said. "It's okay, though. It's been five years. I'm mostly over it."

"Damien might not be."

"What do you mean?"

Alex looked uncomfortable. "I don't know, Elisabeth. Just that…I don't know, his wounds are a little fresher than yours, you know? Maybe this wasn't such a good idea after all."

I frowned. It was odd – now that the idea didn't seem likely at all, I wanted it more than ever. I was starting to hunger for this man in a way I couldn't explain, a way that almost frightened me.

"What's wrong?" Alex reached over and touched my forehead. "You look flushed."

I bit my lip. "Look, I know I don't get real very often and talk about my feelings, but *please* talk to Billy about it. Maybe he'll change his mind. Just tell him what I told you – I'm not looking for anything serious, but I'd love to meet Damien." I flushed. "I know this sounds crazy, but we're like, so compatible. I even looked up his birthday – he's a second-decan Taurus, which means that he'd be perfect for me!"

Alex laughed. "Only you would think of something like that," she said, shaking her head.

"Please?" I put my hands together in front of my chest. "Pretty please with a vodka-soaked cherry on top?"

Alex shook her head, but she was still laughing. "Okay, fine," she said. "I'll talk to him. I promise."

I grinned. "Awesome," I said. "I just know things are going to work out."

Alex eyed me skeptically. "Just don't be heartbroken if they don't," she said.

I laughed. "Trust me, I'm not looking to fall in love. I just want to have a little fun with this gorgeous guy," I added. "Nothing bad will happen."

4

***

Getting Billy to soften on what Alex and I took to calling "The Issue" wasn't easy. At first, his answer was still a firm no. Alex had to work on him for a week, begging and pleading, before he'd even listen to what she had to say without getting red in the face and storming out. I hadn't seen Alex so stressed since she'd first met Billy and fallen in love with him, and I did feel a little guilty for straining their marriage. But at the same time, Alex was totally on board with me. She thought it was a good idea, regardless of whether or not it could help Damien in court. Ever since I'd told her that I was starting to feel like moving on from my trainwreck of a marriage, I knew that she'd be on my side.

Admittedly, the more I thought about it, the more nervous I got. I hadn't dated anyone in quite a while – Jeremy, the disaster from the pottery shop – didn't count. Going out with him was like going out with someone from art class. We'd gotten together for beer, pizza, and sex. I hadn't even had that bad of a time until I realized that Jeremy didn't recognize me at all. Thinking about it now made me roll my eyes. I was ready for a real man, someone like Damien Edwards.

Plus, I somehow knew that he was going to be dynamite in bed.

Another week wore on and still no good news – if anything, Billy was more opposed to the match than ever. He even threatened to drop Damien as a client if Alex wouldn't stop pestering him about it, which would set their hunt for the perfect home back indefinitely. I was starting to think that it would never happen when Alex finally called me, three weeks later, and told me to come over.

"And be nice," Alex hissed into the phone. "Billy's not in a great mood."

My stomach twisted with anxiety. "Then shouldn't we talk about this another time? Like, maybe when he feels better?"

"I'm worried that if we don't take our chance now, there won't be another time," Alex said grimly. "Just come over when you have a minute. And bring some more of that cheese!"

This time, I brought three wheels of Brie and a freshly-baked loaf with me.

Alex and Billy were sitting in the living room, and I joined them, perching nervously on a chair.

"Look, Elisabeth," Billy said. "If we do this – and by *this* I just mean setting the two of you up to meet, nothing more, you have to promise to keep it casual."

I narrowed my eyes. "Why wouldn't I do that?"

Billy sighed and ran a hand through his thick hair. His blue eyes looked tired. Alex was sitting on the couch beside him and she put a hand on Billy's shoulder and squeezed. A sudden pang of guilt hit me in the stomach when I realized just how much tension this had been causing between the two of them.

"Damien has been through a lot," Billy said heavily. "He's really struggling with this. Candace – his wife – cheated on him for years, and he had no idea until someone else in the company told him. Somehow, she managed to convince everyone that she and Damien were in an open relationship. She basically flaunted the affair right under his nose, and he's beatin' the heck out of himself for not seein' it sooner."

"Oh my god," I said. "I can't imagine something as bad as that."

Billy nodded. "He's a little fragile right now," he said. "And I wouldn't want you to get hurt."

I bit my lip. "Why would I get hurt?"

Billy sighed. "Just because, Elisabeth. You're an intense person, you know? Don't go in there expectin' the world, because Damien's just not ready to give it right now."

I nodded. "I am eager to start dating again," I said. "But you know the saying – once burned. I don't think marriage is in my future, no matter how amazing the guy is."

"Yeah," Billy said. "Besides, I gotta say – a quickie engagement on Damien's behalf wouldn't look right to a judge. He'd suspect infidelity, much like Candace, and it could really hurt Damien's case." He sighed again, looking exhausted. "But – and this is an awful big but – if y'all genuinely like each other, it could help."

I nodded. "That's all I want," I said honestly. "I'm really not interested in anything serious right now."

Billy nodded. "Okay," he said. He looked relieved. "I'm glad to see that we're all on the same page here."

"So, when I do get to meet him?"

"I've got a consult with him tomorrow afternoon," Billy said. "I'll bring it up then."

My jaw dropped. "That's so soon," I said. "And you haven't mentioned it before now?"

Billy laughed. "Heck no," he said. He ruffled Alex's black hair affectionately. "In fact, it took until today for my wife to convince me to go through with the darned thing!"

I bit my lip. "What do you think he'll say?"

Billy shrugged. "No clue," he said. "All I know is this – it's really gonna depend on his mood."

I nodded. My stomach was churning with anxiety and my nerves were all on fire, but I couldn't shake the sense of excitement. It felt like being on a really tall rollercoaster, riding towards the top – that moment right before the cars plunge downhill and your stomach feels like it's going to come out of your mouth.

When I got home that night, I couldn't sleep. I spent another obsessive evening glued to my computer, reading everything I could about Damien. In addition to being incredibly successful, he was also a philanthropist – he'd started a foundation for early-childhood education in low-income areas. By the time I went to bed, I was starting to think that maybe all of this was a mistake. Why would Damien want someone like me? Sure, I was successful in my own way – and my pottery always sold whenever I felt like bringing it to the store – but I'd barely finished high school. I hadn't even gone to college! Back when Richard and I had first married, I'd taken some classes at the local community college, but I'd found them so boring and tedious that I'd dropped out before the semester was halfway through.

As loathe as I was to admit it, I couldn't compare with someone like Candace. According to a profile of her, she was one of the wealthiest (and most highly educated) socialites of the south. She had her own charity – a foundation for low-income women who needed professional clothing for interviews – and she'd been interviewed twice by *Town & Garden* magazine, about her gardening, cooking, and how she managed to raise two twin girls.

Of course, I knew that things on paper didn't always reflect in real life. Billy and Alex had painted the image of a shallow, spoiled, and selfish woman. But what if she wasn't? What if Damien was the real villain of their marriage?

How the hell was I supposed to go through with it?

--

Four days later, Alex called.

"Billy met with Damien again and this time, he mentioned you," she said. "Before you get mad, know that he didn't forget the first time. He said Damien was in such a bad mood that he didn't want to bring it up."

My heart skipped a beat and began thudding faster in my chest. "I see," I said slowly.

"But anyway, this time, Damien was in a much better mood. He was intrigued – especially when Billy showed your picture."

I cringed. "Oh, god. Which one?"

Alex laughed. "Elisabeth, relax! It's the one of you in that white cotton dress, posing with some of your pottery. Remember? The one that was in *The Savannah Gazette*."

I bit my lip. "At least that was a flattering one," I mumbled.

"Anyway, Damien wanted to know if you'd be free for dinner tonight. He told Billy to tell you that he wouldn't normally be so spontaneous, but he's going on a trip out of town for the next week or so, and that he wondered if you were free."

I laughed nervously. "I think this is his way of testing me," I said.

"What do you mean?"

"Like, he wants to make sure I'm not high maintenance," I said. "He doesn't want someone who would be put-off by asking for a same-day dinner."

Alex was silent.

"Well?" I raised an eyebrow. "What do you think?"

"I think you're probably right," she said. "So, do you want to go?"

"Yeah," I said. "You can call Billy and tell him to give Damien my number."

Alex laughed. I could tell by the sound of her voice that she was blushing.

"Here's the thing, Elisabeth," she said nervously. "He already made a reservation. He told Billy to tell you to meet him there."

My eyebrows shot up. "He'd do that without even speaking to me?"

"Evidently so," Alex replied. "I was surprised, too."

"So...what are the details?"

"Seven-thirty, at Chez Monique."

"Wow. That's the most expensive restaurant in Savannah. I hope he doesn't think that we're going to go Dutch."

Alex giggled. "Trust me, you have nothing to worry about it," she said.

"Oh, yes I do."

"What's that?"

"What am I going to wear?"

Alex collapsed into laughter. "Stay there," she said. "I'll be right over."

Half an hour later, my bedroom was covered with clothing. Alex stood in front of my closet, her hands on her narrow hips.

"If I were thinner, I'd want something of yours," I moaned enviously. "None of this is going to look good at Chez Monique!"

"Elisabeth, you'll be fine," Alex said kindly. "Everything you have is great. It all suits you."

I buried my face in my hands. "That's the problem," I whined. "None of it is fancy enough!"

"What about this?" Alex held up the white cotton dress I'd worn in the photo Billy had shown Damien. It was a nice dress – probably one of the most flattering things I had – but it dipped low in the front, showing a lot of cleavage.

"I don't know." I wrinkled my nose. "That's kind of a lot for a first date."

Alex glanced at her phone. "Well, you're going to have to pick something soon," she said. "You have to meet him in an hour and a half."

My stomach flipped nervously. "Ugh," I said. "Just pick something, I don't care."

Alex handed me a black dress. It was made of a stretchy material, and even though it was casual, I thought I could dress it up with some heels and makeup. In the end, after adding a bit of jewelry, I thought I looked all right. My hair was endlessly wavy in the humid Savannah heat but I coiled it into a loose chignon, pulling a few tendrils down at my temples and above my ears.

"You look beautiful," Alex said. "He's not going to be able to take his eyes off of you."

I bit my lip. "I look passable," I grumbled.

"Come on, Elisabeth, be nice," Alex said. She smiled encouragingly. "I really think this is going to go well."

I grabbed my purse and nervously spritzed on some sandalwood perfume.

"I hope so," I said. "I haven't been this nervous in a long time."

Alex patted me on the shoulder. "Don't worry about it," she said. "You'll be great. I promise."

I rolled my eyes. "I hope so," I said. "I really do."

The traffic on the way to Chez Monique was terrible, and I knew I was going to be late. I wished that I had Damien's number – at least that way, I could've called him to let him know. But when I called Billy's law office, he'd already left for the day and Alex didn't answer her cell phone. *Besides*, I thought as I pulled up to Chez Monique just after eight o'clock. *I can't rely on Alex and Billy to do everything for me. I'm thirty-three fucking years old. Time to act like it.*

Stepping into the foyer of the restaurant made my nerves come rushing back. I quickly scanned the restaurant, looking Damien's dark head but I didn't see him anywhere. My heart sank. *Great*, I thought. *I'm too late. He must have decided he wasn't going to wait for me and he left.*

"Can I help you?" A perky, beautiful hostess slid in front of me and gave me a dazzling smile. I tried to compose myself.

"Uh, yeah, I'm meeting Damien Edwards. He had a reservation, but I'm late. I didn't have his number or I would've called."

The hostess nodded. There seemed to be a touch of something – envy? curiosity? – in her eyes but she didn't reveal anything.

"This way, please," she said, leading me through the restaurant and towards the back of the large dining room. A beautiful stone fireplace was filled with flowers and delicate tealights flickered on every table. The ambience was astonishing and soothing – I'd never been inside this place, much less thought about what it looked like.

"Here you are," the hostess said sweetly. "Mr. Edwards, your companion is here."

When I saw the back of Damien's dark head, my heart did a somersault in my chest. But when he turned around, I felt my stomach ice over.

"You're late," Damien said coldly.

"I'm really sorry," I said quickly. "There was traffic – I would've called, but Billy didn't give me your number and---"

"I'm not interested in excuses." Damien's dark eyes flashed and a nervous thrill went soaring through my body.

"You're rude."

Damien glared at me. "Not any ruder than tardiness," he said icily.

We stared at each other for a moment. Everything else disappeared around me and I felt myself falling into Damien's dark eyes. In person, he was even more beautiful than his photographs. His skin was pale and perfectly even. His lips were almost as pouty as that of an Old Hollywood starlet. And his dark eyebrows were groomed, framing his eyes with a deep intensity. He was wearing all black – a black button-down shirt, black jacket, and black jeans that weren't too baggy.

"I'm sorry," I said again, flushing hotly. "Are we still on for dinner?"

Damien gave a brief, almost imperceptible nod of his head. He lowered himself into his seat and I bit my lip before joining him at the small table.

"This place looks amazing," I gushed as I picked up a menu. "I've never eaten here before."

"It's the only passable restaurant in Savannah," Damien said. His eyes flicked over the wine list.

"I wouldn't go that far," I said slowly. "I take it you don't like fried seafood?"

"No."

I bit my lip. "Or talking," I mumbled. "I'm guessing you don't really like talking, either."

Damien didn't reply. Another beautiful girl sauntered up to the table and suddenly, he looked up with interest, making no effort to hide the fact that she had amazing tits…at least in his eyes. I felt a hot surge of anger and humiliation.

"Hi, I'm the sommelier," the girl chirped. "What can I get you two to drink?"

"A bottle of Shiraz," Damien said.

"Sorry," I said quickly. "But I hate reds. Could I get a glass of pinot grigio instead, maybe chardonnay?"

"Sure, that's fine, I've got a house char—"

"No," Damien said quickly. His eyes flashed with anger. "We'll just take the Shiraz." He eyed me and a shiver crawled down my spine. "It's excellent," he said. "Even if you don't care for reds."

After the sommelier had walked off – with Damien's gaze clinging to her heart-shaped ass – I stared at him.

"You like to be in charge, huh?"

Damien didn't reply. "The lamb is good here," he said. "I recommend it. Shall I order that for both of us?"

I narrowed my eyes. *What is going on here,* I thought. *Am I really this out of the loop? Has dating totally changed in the last ten years, or what?*

"Sure," I said. I shrugged. "Whatever you want."

Damien settled against the back of his chair. "So, you're a friend of William's."

"His wife's, actually," I said. "We're next door neighbors."

Damien didn't smile. "I see."

"I thought we'd get along," I continued, feeling foolish as the words spilled from my mouth. "I mean, it's not really like I meet a lot of likeminded people in Savannah. I'm not from here originally, I'm from Oregon, and things are really different. I've lived all over those – I was in San Diego for a while before moving here. What about you? You don't have an accent, so either you—"

"And what made you think that we would get along?"

I narrowed my eyes. "You don't know anything about me," I said. "What makes you think we *wouldn't*?"

The tension between us was rolling in thick, heady waves across the table.

Damien shrugged. "I don't get along with a lot of people," he said.

"Obviously," I muttered under my breath.

"And you seem to have a completely different lifestyle than I," Damien continued. "One that perhaps would not be compatible with my own."

I narrowed my eyes. "And what is *that* supposed to mean?"

"You're an artist, aren't you?"

"I make pottery."

"Artistic types often frustrate me," Damien said. "They often have no drive, and I wonder what really motives them."

"Excuse me," I said hotly. "But I've been on my own for the past five years and I've managed to support myself. I'm not some college kid, smoking pot and spending all day laughing at stupid things on the internet!"

Damien narrowed his eyes.

"Besides," I said. "You look like Gomez Addams over there! Try wearing all black and looking as goth as you do without relating to artists, even just a little bit."

Damien's face hardened. The sommelier brought the wine and poured two glasses. She smiled and chattered the whole time, obviously blissfully unaware of the tension building at the small table.

I took a tentative sip of the wine. To my shock, it was actually good.

"This isn't bad," I said, taking another long swallow.

"Yes," Damien said. "I believe I mentioned that."

I sank back against the seat. Damien was both insufferable and intriguing at once – I wondered if he was always like this. How the hell had he managed to snag a wife in the first place?

"I'm grateful to Billy for introducing us," I said. The words hung heavily in the air.

"Yes."

"It's been a long time since I've gone out with anyone," I said, blushing. "I haven't really been looking for anything in years—"

"And just what do you think is going to happen between us?" Damien asked. His eyes flashed in the dim lighting. "Do you think I'm going to ask you to be my girlfriend, to be the mother of my children?"

"I don't—"

"Yes, you don't know," Damien said coldly. "And let me tell you *this*: even if something were to happen between us, it would be ages before I'd even think of introducing you to my girls. They're my family and I need to protect them from all that's wrong in the world."

I stood up, knocking my chair back and glaring hotly. Tears pricked at my eyes and I grabbed my glass of wine. Before I could even think about what I was doing, I dumped it over Damien's head.

"You think I'm what's wrong in the world, seriously?" I shook my head in disgust. "You never even gave me a chance! I've never met a man as rude, self-centered, and entitled as you! And my ex-husband cheated on me for years! At least he was pleasant to speak to," I said angrily, venom dripping from my words. "Fuck you," I spat, before turning on my heel and stalking angrily out of Chez Monique.

I was filled with anger and embarrassment. This hadn't just been a bad idea – it had been the worst idea that Alex and I had ever had. As I drove home, I vowed to erase Damien Edwards from my memory. Staying single for the rest of my life would be preferable to spending just one more minute with that prick, and I never wanted to see him again.

Tears flowed down my face but by now, I was beyond caring. *Fuck him,* I thought. *I don't need to be around someone that insufferable, anyway. He can take his smugness and shove it right up his ass.*

5

***

The next morning, I stalked over to Alex's condo as soon as Billy had left for work. She was obviously surprised to see me, but she put Jacob down in the living room with a "Jacob show" and made a pot of coffee.

"How did it go?" Alex asked cautiously.

I rolled my eyes. "You can tell it went like shit," I said. "I know I look like hell." I'd spent the night crying in bed and I knew that my eyes were bloodshot and my hair was hanging in greasy tangles around my shoulders.

"I was hoping it went well and you just had a hangover," Alex said. She frowned. "What happened?"

I sighed before launching into the whole bloody saga. "It was awful," I said, after I'd finished recounting his boorish behavior, bad manners, and incredibly cruel language. "I've never been so humiliated in my life."

Alex nodded. She gave me a sympathetic smile and reached out to squeeze my shoulder. "I know," she said. "He sounds like a real jerk."

"It was worse than that," I said. "He made me feel subhuman. I didn't ever think a guy could make me feel that bad about myself again, but it was seriously worse than the time Richard told me he was fucking another woman because I had gotten too boring."

"Shh," Alex said, holding a finger to her lips and jerking her head towards the living room. "Little pitchers have big ears."

"Sorry," I mumbled. Normally, I took great pains not to curse when Jacob was in earshot. But today, I couldn't even make myself care.

"He's such a self-righteous jerk," I said. "I don't care what happens to him in court. He can fight his own stupid custody battle, I'm over it."

Alex frowned. "He's going through a lot right now, Elisabeth," she said softly. "Maybe you should give him another chance."

My jaw dropped. "Are you kidding me? After that? It was like seriously, the world's worst date!"

Alex shrugged. "His wife has been cheating on him for years," she said. "He's probably feeling really betrayed. I mean, maybe it changed how he thinks of women."

I bit my lip. "That still doesn't give him any right to treat me that way," I said stiffly. "It was like he was out to humiliate me from the very beginning."

"I know," Alex said quickly. She sipped her coffee. "Look, I'm not saying that he gets a pass for acting like such a nasty person. But maybe he's just not dealing with all of this very well. I mean, it's been a much longer time for you – you've been divorced five years."

"Ouch."

"I didn't mean it like that," Alex said quickly. "Trust me, Elisabeth, I know you're a great woman. But maybe Damien is just soured on the whole experience right now. Maybe he's not ready for you."

"Then he never should've agreed to meet me," I said flatly.

Alex gave me a sympathetic smile. "I guess not," she said. "Look, I've got to run some errands. You wanna come? We can get lunch afterwards," she added. "As long as you don't mind pizza – it's all Jacob wants now."

"Nah," I said. "Tempting, but I should get some work done." I stretched and cracked my knuckles. "There's an exhibition coming up and I should probably make an effort to submit a piece or two."

Alex nodded. "I get that," she said. "If you change your mind, we're leaving in about half an hour."

I drained the last of my coffee, then carried my mug over to Alex's sink and rinsed it out.

"Oh, Elisabeth?"

"Yeah?"

"What should I tell Billy?"

I shrugged. "Whatever you want," I said.

Alex wrinkled her nose. "Really?"

"Yeah," I said. "I really don't care." I shrugged again. Some of the previous night's humiliation came rushing back to me and I flushed.

"Okay. Well, see you."

I waved jauntily as I left and walked back to my own condo. Inside was blissfully quiet and cool. I decided to make a pot of tea, then find some good music and spend the rest of the day in my studio. I know it sounds cliché, but sometimes my best works come from times when I'm not feeling good. After Richard had left, I'd designed a series of clay figures that had sold to a wealthy buyer from India for over six thousand dollars.

It had been, by far, my most successful sell as an artist.

Just as I was pouring my tea and adding lemon and honey, there was a knock at the door. I rolled my eyes. *Geez, Alex,* I thought as I wiped my hands on my jeans and walked into the foyer. *I'm not Jacob, I don't need hand-holding whenever something goes wrong.*

"Alex, really," I said as I opened the door.

I gasped.

Damien was standing there, a large bouquet of fragrant peonies in his arms. Despite the beautiful floral offering, he seemed no more cheerful than he had the previous night. Unfortunately, he still looked just as gorgeous. His dark hair gleamed in the sun and his mouth was twisted into a sexy scowl.

"These are for you," Damien said shortly.

I narrowed my eyes. "You can't be serious," I replied. "Why the hell would you bring my flowers?"

Damien thrust the bouquet into my hands. When his fingers brushed mine, an electric shock ripped through my body. My breath caught in my throat and my heart skipped a beat. We locked eyes.

"You should come in," I murmured. "I'll put these in some water."

Damien stepped closer, bridging the gap between our bodies. I shivered as he reached out and pushed a piece of hair behind my ear. His dark eyes shone with intensity. My stomach twisted with anxiety and something warm, something liquid, as Damien licked his lips and stared at me.

"What?" I asked softly.

Damien didn't reply. He leaned forward and before I could realize what he was doing, pressed his lips to mine. The flowers crushed against my chest as he stepped closer and wrapped his arms around my waist, pulling me roughly against his body. I let out a small yelp of pleasure as Damien twined his hands around my body, squeezing my ass through my jeans.

Arousal exploded in my lower belly and I whimpered. Damien pushed me inside and kicked the door closed behind us. Our kiss didn't break as I dropped the flowers and wrapped my arms around Damien's neck. My heart was pounding but lust was flowing through my body. I'd never been as attracted to anyone as I was to Damien, and even though I knew this was a catastrophically bad idea, I didn't care. I wanted him.

Damien shoved me against a wall, probing my mouth with his tongue and nibbling my lower lip until I moaned softly into his mouth. I purred, pressing my body against his lean mass, enjoying the feel of his muscular chest through his soft black t-shirt. Up close, he smelled like whiskey and leather and I swooned as I inhaled his personal fragrance. Damien scooped me up and I wrapped my legs around his waist. Without taking his lips from mine, Damien carried me through the house and into my bedroom where he dropped me on the bed.

Damien's dark eyes were fiery with lust. He

stared down at me, licking his lips and unfastening his belt. I fumbled with the snap of my jeans, pulling them down my thighs. Before I could reach for my shirt, Damien crawled on top of my body and pinned me to the bed. He straddled my torso and I moaned as he covered my neck and collarbone with a line of scorching hot kisses. Arousal flowed through my veins like honey as Damien reached under my shirt and began rolling my stiff nipples between his fingers. It felt so good that tears came to my eyes and I moaned, arching my back, wanting more.

Damien ripped my shirt away, pulling the shreds of fabric away from my body until I was topless underneath him. He kept his fierce gaze locked with mine as he crossed his arms over his chest and pulled his shirt off. I gasped – he was so beautiful, moreso than I ever could have imagined. His chest was sleek but toned, with a light smattering of black hair threaded with silver. My mouth watered as I watched his muscles ripple. He unzipped his jeans and climbed off me as he tossed them to the side. Before I could move, Damien was back on the bed, his hand between my legs and his other arm pulling me into a passionate kiss.

I moaned loudly into Damien's mouth as his fingers touched me through my jeans. Squirming and moaning, I wriggled closer, eager for more of his touch. My clit was swollen and hard and I could feel that I was soaking my panties with arousal. The room was filled with a musky blend of my own scent and Damien's, and I closed my eyes as I reveled in the sensual mix. Damien yanked my jeans down my hips and tossed them to the side. When I was clad only in a thong, he smirked at me.

I licked my lips. Damien pushed me down and crawled between my legs. He grabbed both of my wrists with one hand, pinning my hands over my head, and began teasing my breasts with his mouth. He stuck his tongue out and licked at my stiff nipples until I was begging for more, then gently nipped the tender flesh and made me cry out with intense pleasure.

"God," I moaned, closing my eyes and arching my back. Damien slipped his hand inside of my panties and began kneading my clit until stars were exploding before my eyes. When he leaned against my body, I could feel his arousal through the thin material of his black boxers. It was enough to make me gasp – he was obviously huge!

Fumbling and struggling against Damien, I managed to free my hands. I reached for him, stroking his hard cock through his boxer shorts. Damien groaned. He pressed my hand against his erection and thrust his hips, obviously enjoying himself. I smirked. *Not so haughty now, are you*, I thought as I rubbed his cock. *Now that you're getting some attention, you're actually not so bad.*

Damien growled. He yanked his boxers down, then crawled between my legs and bent over my torso. He nipped and kissed my stomach and I moaned as his mouth moved lower and lower. I spread my legs and pushed my hips forward. My pussy was on fire as Damien moved skillfully down my body. When he was between my thighs, he looked up at me and raised his eyebrows.

"Want something?" Damien asked with a smirk.

I flushed hotly. "I think you know."

Damien bit his lip. He didn't break eye contact with me as he kissed the inside of my thigh. A shiver of lust crawled down my spine and a moan escaped my lips as he finally turned his attention to my secret place. As Damien gently flicked my clit with his tongue, I buried my hands in his silky dark hair and tugged at his scalp. Damien purred into me, slipping a finger inside of me and wriggling it as his lips fastened around my clit and began to suck. Intensely pleasurable sensations raced through my body and I groaned, grinding my hips against his face, wanting more.

Damien pulled away and I groaned. He climbed up my body and kissed me wetly. I licked my own arousal off his lips and tongue as Damien kneeled between my legs and ran his hands up and down my body. Every inch of my skin was tingling with anticipation and arousal as Damien's cock pressed against my soaked labia.

"Are you clean?" Damien whispered in my ear.

I reached into my nightstand and fumbled around, praying that I still had a few condoms. Thankfully, my fingers brushed against a foil square and I handed it to Damien. He ripped it open with his teeth, sheathing his cock in latex and steadying himself with a hand against my thigh.

Damien locked eyes with me, then thrust deeply inside. I screamed with pleasure and wrapped my legs around his waist, riding him from underneath. Damien thrust in deeply to the hilt, then began to rock back and forth. As our bodies moved together, his pubic bone brushed my clit and I shuddered with pleasure.

I buried my face in Damien's neck and moaned as he made love to me. His breath was hot on my body and he tangled his fingers in my hair, pulling my neck back.

"You'd look so hot tied up," Damien whispered in my ear. "I'd love to fuck you, just take my time with you and make you beg for sweet release."

His thrilling words sent lust shooting through my body and I groaned with pleasure. As Damien's thrusts grew more intense, I could feel my orgasm building in my lower belly.

"You like that," Damien growled. "You like the idea of being my little fucktoy?"

I whimpered with pleasure and my cheeks burned bright red. I'd never had anyone speak to me like this before in bed, but I couldn't deny that I found it hotter than I could have possibly imagined.

"Yeah," I moaned in Damien's ear. "Make me yours."

Without sliding out of me, Damien reached to the side of the bed and came up with his belt. He grinned and folded it into a loop, gently smacking the side of my thigh as he rode me. I yelped – but somehow, the slight pain only mingled with the pleasure racing through my body and made it more intense.

Damien grabbed my wrists and twined them together in his belt, looping it roughly over the headboard of my bed. When I tried to pull my arms free, I found that I couldn't. Damien grinned down at me. He ran his hands down my chest, pinching and tweaking at my nipples until the flesh was puckered and stiff. It felt so good that I could hardly stand it.

Damien began thrusting harder than ever, until his body was slamming against mine. He grabbed my ankles and hauled my legs over his shoulders, penetrating me deeply. I moaned with pleasure as he slipped a hand between my legs and began thumbing my clit to the rhythm of his strokes. Soon, my orgasm was crashing over me like a tidal wave. I closed my eyes and grunted, moaning and straining as the thrilling, gripping sensation flooded my body again and again.

"God," Damien growled. He closed his eyes and moved against me, slamming his hips against mine. He sucked in his breath and groaned loudly. I shivered with pleasure as his cock twitched inside of me. When he came, he kissed me hard, penetrating my mouth with his tongue until all I could taste was Damien.

For a few seconds, we lay there, panting and entwined. Then Damien reached for the headboard and unfastened my wrists, gently rubbing where his belt had chafed my tender skin. He grinned at me, then slid out.

I stretched and pulled the sheet over my naked hips. Damien didn't make eye contact as he reached for his boxers, then his pants, his shirt, and finally, his belt. As he dressed, I couldn't help but feel vulnerable that I was still naked.

"Thanks for the flowers," I said in a shaky voice. My body was still trembling from the intense pleasure I'd just experienced. "They're beautiful."

"I think I owe you a new shirt," Damien said. He raised his eyebrow and pulled his wallet from his pocket. "Does three hundred work?"

"Oh, god, no, don't worry about it," I said quickly. The thought of taking his money was incredibly humiliating.

"No, I insist," Damien said. He pulled a few crisp hundreds from his wallet and tucked them on the nightstand. I rolled my ideas, thinking that I'd hand the cash over to Billy and tell him to put it towards Damien's legal fees.

I swallowed. The air between us was still thick and tense – oddly, the round of incredible sex had done nothing to change that. Damien stared at me and I stared back, expecting him to speak. Instead, he turned on his heel and walked out of my apartment.

Bastard, I thought as the door slammed shut. *What a jerk! He didn't even want to talk to me! He just…showed up, fucked me, and left!*

But I couldn't deny that I was more attracted to him than I'd ever thought possible. He was my perfect ideal – dark, brooding, and sexy.

Too bad he was also a huge jerk.

Oh well, I told myself as I finally climbed out of bed. *At least he was good in bed*.

6

***

The rest of the weekend felt like a real wash. After having a wild romp with Damien, I wasn't in the mood to create. Instead, I opened a bottle of wine and relaxed with a movie. I couldn't keep from thinking about him...and I certainly wasn't going to rush over to Alex's and spill what had just happened.

Richard always used to say that I hated being wrong. I'd never liked hearing that, but the older I got, the more I thought that maybe, just maybe, he'd been right. At least, about that one thing, anyway.

On Monday morning, I got up and spent a few hours in the studio. But I couldn't focus. Sitting at my wheel, elbow-deep in clay, I couldn't stop thinking about Damien. Finally, I gave up. I put my clay away, washed my tools, then spent fifteen minutes scrubbing the clay from under my fingernails. I knew I was stalling, but I couldn't help it. I was nervous – it had been years since I'd actually liked someone.

And I certainly wasn't going to let myself get hurt.

I settled down with my phone and a diet soda. It took over five minutes for me to work up the courage to dial the number.

"Hello, thanks so much for calling Global Visions. This is Anna, how may I help you?"

I coughed. "Uh, yeah, I'd like to speak with Damien Edwards."

"I'm sorry, who?"

I squinted. "The CEO of the company. Damien Edwards."

Anna, or whatever her name was, giggled nervously. "I'm sorry, ma'am, I don't have any information about the upper management. Would you like to speak to someone in sales?"

"No," I said shortly. *Shit!* I thought. *How the hell am I supposed to reach him?*

"I can give you our directory information," Anna chirped brightly. "I'll direct you now."

"Wait, I—"

Beep!

"Thank you for calling Global Visions. If you know the extension of your party, you may dial it at any time. For the directory, please punch in the first three letters of your party's last name." The mechanical voice was both patronizing and sweet.

I groaned, then tapped the keys for 'EDW.'

"Eddlesworth, Hannah, extension one-fifty-four. Edgerton, Joyce, extension two-eighty-six. Ellsworth, Anna, extension four-ninety-four. Exeter, Allen, extension two-ninety-eight. If none of these people are your correct party, please press zero to return to the main menu."

"Fuck," I groaned. I hung up.

Taking a sip of my drink, I dialed the general number once again."

"Thank you for calling Global Visions, this is Randolph. How may I direct your call?"

"Yeah," I said. "I'd like to speak to the executive secretary."

"May I have your name, please?"

I bit my lip. "Yeah, this is Elisabeth Tessoro, I'm with a vendor."

"Oh, okay. One second, please."

Yes! I thought. *Triumph!*

Randolph put me on hold, then transferred me.

"Hello, this is Olivia. How may I help you?"

Thinking fast, I said: "Hi, this is Elisabeth, I'm calling for Damien. I work for his lawyer."

"Oh! Billy just called," Olivia said. "I bet he forgot something, didn't he?"

I blushed. "Yeah," I said. "I won't be long."

"Damien's in his office now, I'll patch you right through."

I grinned. *Perfect.*

"This is Damien."

"Hey, it's me," I said. "Elisabeth."

Damien laughed. The sound was startling, and I blushed even harder when I realized that it was the first time I'd heard him laugh.

"How the hell did you get here?" Damien

snickered. "Most people couldn't get through to me if they tried all day."

"Oh, you know, natural luck," I said.

"I like that," Damien growled.

A shiver soared through my body. "Look," I said. "Maybe we got off on the wrong foot. Yesterday was…fun," I added lamely, unable to think of a better word. "I'd like to have dinner with you again."

"Oh yeah?" Damien's voice was both sarcastic and amused, and I shivered again, remembering the way he'd made me come.

"Yeah," I replied. I swallowed. "You free on Thursday night?"

Damien chuckled. "Don't you know that men are supposed to do the asking?"

"Clearly not," I said dryly. "I'm a hippie chick, we aren't allowed to buy into social norms."

Damien snickered. "Okay, then," he said. "Meet me at eight on Thursday night, at The Loft."

My mouth went dry. I wouldn't have admitted it,

but a part of me had been afraid Damien would say no.

"Cool," I managed to say. "I'll see you there."

"Elisabeth?"

"Yeah?"

"I'm looking forward to seeing you."

The line went dead before I could reply. My stomach was all fluttery and my skin felt hot, almost like my diet soda had really been four glasses of wine in one. And when I stood up, I realized that I was wet.

Damnit, I thought good-naturedly. A shiver ran down my spine. *What am I doing with this guy?*

The rest of the week crawled by. I spent Tuesday in my studio, then gave a free lecture on pottery on Wednesday down at the pottery shop. Normally, I lived for those little gatherings. But instead, it just made me feel antsy and impatient, like I was killing time before the main event.

By the time it was seven-thirty on Thursday, I was breathless and ready to go. I spent extra time getting ready – this time, I chose a form-fitting black cocktail dress, heels, and a lot of black eyeliner. I certainly wasn't going to make the same mistake twice.

The Loft was beautiful – Savannah's first organic gourmet restaurant, it had been around for over twenty years. The inside was understated and cozy with exposed brick walls, lots of brass and dark wood, and clean, minimal lighting.

When he saw me, Damien raised an eyebrow and smirked. I blushed hotly. Before I could lower myself into the chair, he got up and pulled it away from the table for me.

"Thanks," I said softly.

Damien kissed me on the back of the neck and I shuddered.

As he sat down across from me, I could feel the air begin to thicken with tension.

"How are you?" I asked lamely. I felt so strange whenever I was around Damien – normally, I'm incredibly chatty, but somehow our silences felt more poignant than any conversation could. *It's because he's so intense*, I thought. *Hearing him speak almost seems unnatural.*

Damien took a long swallow of water. "I'm thinking of starting with the vintage oak-aged Chardonnay," Damien said. "That sound good?"

I nodded.

"That was really something, how you got to me at work," Damien added. He raised an eyebrow. "Not many people could have done that."

I bit my lip and shrugged. "Quick thinking, I guess," I said.

"Evidently," Damien replied.

"So…" I trailed off. "What do you do when you're not working?"

"Not much, to be honest," Damien said. "Mostly I take care of my girls. They don't see their mother very often, and they're at that age where they need a lot of attention."

I nodded. "I don't have children," I said. "But I babysit my best friend's son all the time. You know Alex, Billy's wife?"

Damien nodded. "Yeah. Billy's got a photo of him on his desk at work."

We lapsed into silence once again. Thankfully, the waiter approached and Damien gave our wine order, as well as an order of chipotle brie bites and white bean hummus with truffle oil.

"That sounds good." I narrowed my eyes. "You didn't even look at the menu!"

Damien laughed and a shiver ran down my spine. "I didn't need to," he said easily. "I've been coming here for years. That's the only reason I knew they'd have a table for us tonight. I'm probably their best customer."

I looked around. "Now that you mention it, this is probably the best spot," I said. Damien and I were nestled into a dark corner, with an antique oil lamp hanging on the wall. His face in the shadows looked pale and slender, almost like that of a vampire.

"I took Candace here, for our first date," Damien said calmly.

I frowned. "Why would you tell me that?" I narrowed my eyes. If this was suddenly turning into our disastrous first date, I wanted nothing to do with it. Reaching for my purse, I got to my feet and glared at Damien.

"Wait, Elisabeth," Damien said. He wrapped his long fingers around my wrist, holding me in place.

"What?" I blinked. "That was really hurtful, Damien."

"I told you because I don't want there to be secrets between us," Damien said in a deep, intense voice. "I'm telling you because I realize that I have to start moving on from my disaster of a marriage. I want you to stay, Elisabeth. I like you. I feel a connection with you."

I stared at him, openmouthed.

"Tell me, Elisabeth, do you feel the same way?" Damien's voice was dark and urgent.

I could hardly breathe as I lowered myself down into my chair and nodded slowly.

"Yes," I whispered. "I do."

Damien was still holding my hand. He squeezed, then dipped his head to my fingers and gently turned my hand over in his, kissing my palm. Warmth and arousal spread through my body and I sighed softly.

"I don't know what I'm looking for," I said quietly. "I haven't had a serious relationship since my marriage ended."

Damien nodded. "Neither have I."

I laughed, thinking he was joking. But when his face stayed solemn, I realized he'd been sincere.

"Oh, of course not," I said quickly.

"I don't know what it is that I'm searching for either, Elisabeth," Damien said. "But I feel as though I'd like to explore whatever it is with you."

I nodded slowly. "Me, too," I said in a soft voice. "Me, too."

7

***

"Are you nervous?" Damien raised an eyebrow at me.

"Should I be?" I laughed anxious. The truth was, I was insanely nervous – today was the day Damien was taking me to meet his daughters, Arabella and Annaliese. It had been four months since we'd started seeing each other…and I was starting to feel like I was really falling for him.

"They're intense little girls," Damien said. He steered the black Porsche towards the curb. "But they should like you."

I bit my lip. I'd never really felt like I was good around kids. Jacob was an obvious exception, but he was so easy most of the time that I didn't notice. Most of the time, I couldn't tell whether or not kids wanted me to take them seriously. Was I supposed to squat down to their height and make jokes, or should I just treat them little adults?

Damien reached for my thigh and squeezed. "You'll be great," he said. "You're very easy to get along with."

This time, I laughed for real. "That's pretty rich coming from you," I said slyly. "I take it you've already forgotten that glass of wine I threw in your face."

Damien laughed. "No," he said. "But I deserved it. Trust me."

"Oh, I know," I said. "You were such an asshole."

Damien pushed the car into park and pulled me into a deep embrace. He kissed me passionately, stroking my back with his large, capable hands.

"Just relax and be yourself," Damien said. "It's only an afternoon. I'm sure we'll be fine."

I waited in the car as Damien went inside his house and relieved the babysitter. Minutes later, he appeared with two little brunettes in tow. I snickered when I saw them – Annaliese and Arabella were the spitting image of their father, down to the little smirks on their faces. Like Damien, they had pale skin, dark eyes, and silky dark hair.

Damien opened the back seat and the two girls obediently climbed into their booster seats.

"Hello," one of them said solemnly. "I'm Arabella."

"Hi, Arabella," I said. "I like your barrettes. Bats are one of my favorite animals."

Arabella giggled, then touched the bat-shaped barrette in her dark hair. "Me, too," she said shyly. "Annaliese is afraid of them. She's worried they'll get stuck in her hair."

"Am not!" Annaliese cried. "I'm Annaliese," she said in a loud, bossy voice. "And I'm the older twin."

"You are not!" Arabella cried.

"Am too," Annaliese argued. "By three minutes!"

"It's very nice to meet you, Annaliese," I said. Like Arabella, she was clad in dark purple clothing. But she had a slight smattering of freckles across her nose, and a silver necklace shaped like a ladybug.

Annaliese blushed and looked down in her lap.

"Annaliese, what do we say to Elisabeth?"

"Thank you," Annaliese whispered.

"She's shy," Damien mouthed to me. I nodded.

"So, girls, what would you like to do today?" Damien smiled at his kids, turning his body in the seat as he started the car.

"I don't know," they responded in unison.

"Elisabeth?" Damien turned to me with one brow raised. "Any ideas?"

"Oh, I don't know," I said lamely. "The movies? Lunch?"

"I'm hungry," Arabella announced solemnly.

"Lunch it is then," Damien said. "Where to?"

There was a flurry of whispers from the backseat as the twins consulted each other.

I had to struggle to keep from giggling. It wasn't just that both girls resembled Damien physically, but their serious little demeanors were a perfect copy of his intense behavior.

"Dad, we want cheeseburgers," Annaliese said. "Is that okay?"

"Sounds good to me," Damien said. He turned to me. "Elisabeth?"

"Oh, yeah, great," I said. I expected Damien to drive us to one of the fast food restaurants peppered around Savannah, but instead he drove out of town and parked in front of what looked like a vintage-style dinner.

"I've never been here before," I said to the girls as I climbed out of the car. "What's good?"

Arabella shrugged and blushed, hiding her face in her hands. Annaliese stood tall and tossed her hair.

"I like everything," she said solemnly.

"Cool," I replied, feeling awkward.

Damien ushered the girls inside and an older uniformed waitress squatted down, beaming at the twins – it was obviously a favorite restaurant of theirs. Once we were seated, Damien ordered a basket of fried mushrooms for the table and milkshakes for all four of us.

Arabella relaxed a little, now that she was in a familiar environment. Soon we were chatting about school – when she told me that art was her favorite class, I told her about my pottery and even offered to help her learn to throw pots.

Damien gave me an amused smile as both girls excused themselves to visit the bathroom.

"You're a pro at this," he said. "I hope you're not feeling uncomfortable." He glanced around. "This place is pretty bad, but the girls love it. They won't eat a burger unless it comes out of that kitchen."

I laughed. "I was the same way when I was their age, I only liked fast-food burgers. Whenever my dad would grill, I wouldn't eat them because I didn't like the char."

Damien laughed. "Arabella is the same way," he said. "She's…the pickier one, I'd say."

I shrugged. "They're both so well adjusted and mature," I said. "I've never met five-year-olds before, at least, not any as articulate as your girls."

Damien nodded. "I have tried to do a good job," he said. "It's hard sometimes." He frowned and shook his head. "I don't mean to speak ill of their mother, but she's not a good role model. Sometimes I'm worried they'll both grow up and think that it's normal to act the way she does."

"I hope I wasn't overstepping when I offered Arabella the chance to learn pottery," I said.

Damien shook his head. "Nah, it'd be good for both of them to find hobbies. I've been looking for camps next year, but Annaliese is terrified at the idea of sleeping away from home."

I nodded. "I don't blame her," I said. "I hate sleeping anywhere other than my own bed."

Damien smirked and raised an eyebrow. "Oh, really?" He asked coyly.

I blushed at his innuendo. Just as I was about to reply with something sexy, the girls returned and scooted into their side of the booth.

"Elisabeth had a good idea for after lunch," Damien said. "She said it might be fun to go to the park and feed the ducks, what do you think?"

"Yay!" Annaliese cheered. "I love the park!"

Arabella smiled and nodded.

I leaned against the back of the booth and sipped at my milkshake, finally feeling a little relaxed. I hadn't expected today to go so well, but it seemed that I was really on the right track to a good relationship with Arabella and Annaliese.

By the time we were finished eating, I was starting to feel more comfortable. Arabella and Annaliese had come out of their shells a little bit – at least, enough for me to take a breath every now and then.

"Maybe Elisabeth can watch us, Daddy," Arabella remarked as we walked to the car together. "You know. When you have another one of your dinners."

Damien laughed. He eyed me over the girls' heads, rolling his eyes.

"Maybe," Damien said. He helped both girls into the backseat and then closed the door. "I can't exactly tell her that my *dinners* were dinners with you," Damien added slyly under his breath. "At least, not yet."

I blushed. "I bet," I said archly.

Damien drove us all to the park. The two of us lagged behind as Arabella and Annaliese flew over the grass and scattered handfuls of frozen corn kernels towards the ducks. After a few seconds, the ducks began to eat and Arabella shrieked excitedly. She ran towards Damien and me, flinging kernels everywhere.

"My teacher says it's bad to feed the ducks bread," Arabella said proudly, standing tall. Her dark hair was frizzing out in little wisps all over her face and her cheeks were pink with excitement.

"That's exactly right," I said. "It's always better to give them corn, or lettuce, or frozen peas. Bread makes them sick."

Arabella nodded. "I know," she said bossily. "But Annaliese didn't!"

Before I could reply, Arabella raced towards her sister. Damien kept one careful eye on both girls as he and I strolled around the edge of the water.

"They're going to be exhausted when I take them home," Damien said. He smirked. "At least Candace won't have to worry about actually watching them for once." A trace of bitterness seeped into his tone. "That woman only cares about herself."

I sighed. "I can't imagine what it must be like to co-parent with an ex," I said softly. "Richard and I had always talked about having kids. We even tried – for like, a couple of years. But it never worked and then I found out that he'd secretly gotten a vasectomy."

Damien's eyes went wide. "You're kidding," he said darkly. "What an ass."

I nodded. "Yeah," I said slowly. "But like I said, it's probably easier."

Damien sighed. "I love my girls more than anything else in this world," he said. His eyes flashed with intensity. "But I sometimes wish I had full custody. It would be too much for me alone. But maybe someday."

I nodded again. I felt awkward – there wasn't really anything I could say to that. Even though we'd been seeing each other for a few months, I knew that things between Damien and I weren't exactly serious. Meeting his girls was a huge first step, but it wasn't like he was going to ask me to move in.

The food and time in the sun had made me oddly sleepy, and I closed my eyes as Damien drove. Arabella and Annaliese chattered quietly in the back seat, and the sound was surprisingly soothing. For a moment, I almost felt like we were a family.

Damien slowed to a stop in front of a large, beautiful home. It was more opulent than any of the other homes on the street, with a red brick exterior, black shutters, and copper accents.

"Wow," I said quietly. "This is gorgeous."

Damien nodded. "I bought this house for Candace, but she isn't satisfied," he said in a low voice. "I think it's perfect, but she wants more."

"Oh." I nodded. "I see."

"Daddy, thank you for lunch," Annaliese said. She unbuckled her seat belt and started to climb out of the car.

"Yeah, Dad," Arabella said. "Thanks." She looked at me and cocked her head to the side. "It was nice to meet you, Elisabeth."

I grinned. "It was nice to meet you, too," I said. "And remind your dad about pottery, okay? He can bring you by sometime and I'll show you the basics."

Arabella flushed and dipped her head. "Thank you," she muttered quietly before unfastening her belt and climbing out of the car.

"I'll just be a minute," Damien said. He checked to make sure the girls weren't watching, then leaned in and kissed me gently. I blushed and purred as Damien's lips pressed against mine. When he pulled away, I felt a yank in my lower belly. *I want him*, I thought as I watched his lean form move across the yard and gather his girls. *What is happening to me?*

Damien was inside for ten minutes. When he came out, his mouth was pressed into an angry white line and his dark eyes were flashing.

"What's wrong?" I asked cautiously as he climbed behind the wheel.

"Nothing." Damien scowled as he jammed the key into the ignition. He drove down the street and parked in a cul-de-sac, facing the woods.

"This is a new development," I said, craning my neck. "It's nice."

Damien nodded.

Before I could ask what was really bothering him, he reached across the seat and grabbed my face. With both hands on my cheeks, Damien slipped his tongue into my mouth. I moaned softly as he sucked on my lower lip.

"God, I want you," Damien growled. He unfastened my seatbelt, then pulled me into the backseat. For a moment, all I could do was kiss back, as frantically as passionately as possible. Then my brain clicked on and I gently pulled away.

"Damien, it's the middle of the afternoon," I hissed. "People could see us!"

Damien smirked. "Let them," he said.

I blushed hotly. "I've never done anything like this in public before."

Damien dipped his head to mine and kissed me. He nudged my head up and covered my neck with tiny, thrilling bites that made me moan with arousal. Every nerve in my body was tingling as Damien pushed me down onto the seat and straddled me. I groaned as I felt his hard erection through his pants.

"It turns you on, doesn't it," Damien growled. He pulled my shirt over my head and tossed it to the side before unfastening my bra and biting gently at my stiff nipples. The sensation of his warm teeth and tongue over my sensitive skin was thrilling and I tangled my hair and arched my back, moaning loudly.

"Tell me, Elisabeth," Damien urged. "Tell me how much you want me. Tell me how wet you are."

Flushing hotly, I whimpered my assent. Damien unzipped my jeans and slid two fingers inside my panties, rubbing my crotch until I was grinding my hips against his touch. I wanted more – I wanted to be naked, writhing beneath him as he fucked me.

Biting my lip, I moaned softly as Damien tugged my jeans and panties down my thighs. He left them bunched around my ankles and gently slapped the inside of my thigh. My bare ass against the leather car seat felt lewd and arousing and I knew that my face was burning with a hot flush. Damien fumbled with his belt, shoving his jeans down his hips.

"I'm ready this time," Damien growled. He reached into the center console and pulled out a foil-wrapped condom. I swallowed, panting hard as he ripped the packet open with his teeth and sheathed his cock in a thin layer of latex.

Damien crawled between my legs and stroked a finger down my wet pussy. I moaned as his fingertip brushed against my clit. Damien raised an eyebrow, smirking down at me.

"You like that?"

I bit my lip and nodded, whimpering as he slid a finger inside of me and began to brush against my G-spot. Moaning, I arched my back and spread my thighs as far as I could. The jeans around my ankles constrained my movements, but I had a feeling Damien enjoyed watching me struggle. He grabbed both of my wrists with his free hand and pinned them above my head. As he fingered me, Damien leaned over my body and kissed my stomach before gently sucking on my nipples. Pleasure exploded in my body and I moaned again, begging for more.

When Damien took his hand away, I cried out in frustration. He grinned down at me before grabbing my hips and releasing my arms. I buried my fingers in his hair, tangling and tugging at his scalp until Damien growled with obvious pleasure. As the head of his hard cock poked against my wet labia, I shivered with anticipation.

"You want me?" Damien growled. "Tell me, Elisabeth – I want to hear it from you."

I blushed and nodded. "Yes," I purred softly. "I want you."

Damien steadied himself against my hip, then slid inside of me, burying his cock to the hilt. We groaned in unison as he plunged deep inside of me, slamming his hips against mine with unreal force. I panted and groaned, straining against Damien's lean bulk.

He grinned down at me, moving his hips in a slow, delicious, torturous circle. Each time Damien's body kissed mine, my clit throbbed with exquisite agony. I closed my eyes and moaned, wrapping my arms around Damien's neck and pulling him down close on top of me.

"Oh, yeah," Damien groaned. "God, yes."

I pressed my sweaty cheek against Damien's and began grinding my body against his, desperate for more. Damien's thrusts became deeper and more intense as we moved together and soon I was crying out as a powerful orgasm ripped through my body.

Damien panted and groaned. Sweat dripped from his pale forehead onto my chest and I lay back in a haze of pleasure as he fucked me harder and deeper. My muscles were tight and tingling from my orgasm but it still felt amazing. I was so wet that the seat underneath of my hips was soaking wet and the inside of the car was filled with the musky scent of sex.

"Oh, god," Damien groaned. He nipped at my neck, harder than before, and I cried out in delight as he slammed his hips against mine. When I felt his cock twitching and pulsing inside of my body, I smiled happily. Damien's body strained and thrust. He arched his back, tossing his dark mane over his head and sending a spray of sweat all over my body. I relished the powerful intimacy between us – never had I been with someone this passionate, this frenzied.

When he was finally finished, Damien lay against me and closed his eyes. He was breathing hard and I pushed his sweaty hair away from his pale forehead.

"That was incredible," Damien murmured. He wrapped an arm around me and squeezed me tightly.

I giggled nervously. "And I don't think anyone saw us."

Damien's lips curled into a smirk but he still didn't open his eyes. "Who cares," he murmured. "We were having too much fun to notice, anyway."

I grinned. "Yeah," I said softly.

Soon, the humid air inside of the car began to

chill. Damien pulled away, pulling up his jeans and fastening his belt before climbing into the passenger seat. I was barely able to pull up my own pants and fix my shirt, but putting on my bra would have to wait until I got home. I blushed as I tucked the item into my purse, hoping that I could make it inside without being seen by Alex.

Damien reached for my hand and laced his fingers with mine. "Elisabeth," he said in a low voice. "I think I'm falling in love with you."

My jaw dropped and I whipped my head to face him. "What?"

Damien chuckled, once. "I think you heard me," he said.

I nodded, flushing hotly. "I did," I said softly. "I think I'm falling in love with you, too."

Damien squeezed my hand once more before pulling away and starting the car. As he drove me home, we sat in silence – but it wasn't awkward at all. If anything, I just felt more comfortable with him than ever before. I could practically see the cartoon hearts floating around my head and I bit my lip.

I'd never felt a connection with any man before the way I felt with Damien.

But somehow, I wondered if it was all too good to be true.

8

***

By the end of the following week, I *knew* I was falling in love. Damien and I saw each other every single day – we even had dinner with his girls on Tuesday and Friday. Saturday, he spent the night for the first time. And Sunday, we'd gone to the farmer's market and strolled for hours among the stalls, picking out fresh loaves of jalapeno cheddar ciabatta and the perfect tomatoes for a caprese salad.

We hadn't talked about what we "were" yet, but honestly, I was expecting Damien to bring it up at almost any time. His divorce was nearly settled – Billy was working solid sixty-hour weeks trying to advocate for him – and I couldn't wait to think about what would happen when he was technically a free man.

Not that I was expecting a ring, or anything. But being able to call Damien my boyfriend would be satisfying.

I just knew it.

On Tuesday, I spent the morning in my studio, throwing pots. By the time one o'clock rolled around, I was starving. I thought it would be nice if I could surprise Damien with lunch – I knew that he'd been in a stressful meeting for most of the morning – so I ordered a spread from a Greek deli downtown and called his office.

"Thank you for calling Global Visions, this is Mariah, how may I help you?"

"Hi, Mariah, please patch me through to Olivia, the executive secretary."

There was a pause. I frowned. Normally, whenever I called Damien at work, everyone seemed to know me.

"I'm sorry, ma'am, may I please have your name?"

I rolled my eyes. "It's Elisabeth Tessoro, I need to speak with Damien."

"I'm sorry?"

"Damien Edwards," I said impatiently. "You know. The CEO!"

Mariah cleared her throat. "I'm sorry, Mr. Edwards has asked not to be disturbed for the rest of the day."

I frowned. "He'd be happy to hear from me," I said. "We're personally acquainted."

"I'm sorry, Mr. Edwards has left strict orders not to disturb him today."

I rolled my eyes. "Whatever," I said. "Thanks for nothing."

When I hung up with the inept receptionist, I called Damien's personal cell. To my surprise, it went straight to voicemail. A knot formed in my stomach and I licked my lips.

"Hi, Damien, it's Elisabeth. Look I was hoping you were free for lunch today, but I couldn't get through to you. Call me back, okay?"

I hung up, expecting to hear back within a few minutes.

But the whole afternoon passed with no word at all.

The next day, I tried calling again. My heart sank when I got the same response. I even tried lying again, and saying that I worked for Billy's firm. But this time, my trick didn't work and I stood there, clenching the phone in my hand and shaking with anxiety.

Damien's personal cell went to voicemail.

For four more days in a row.

By the weekend, I was losing my mind. Just as I was pouring myself a lunchtime mimosa, there was a knock on the door. *Oh my god, it's him*, I thought, glancing in the mirror and running my hands through my hair. *I'm still mad but at least he turned up! At least he still cares about me!*

Yanking the door open, I couldn't help slumping in defeat when I saw Alex standing there, holding a box of cupcakes.

"You've never been this unhappy to see me," Alex said awkwardly. "What's going on?"

I sighed and buried my face in my hands. "I'm sorry," I said. "I was…well, I was hoping you were Damien."

Alex pushed past me and shut the door. "What happened? Did you two have a fight?"

"No," I said sadly. I walked into the kitchen and sat down at the table, taking a greedy sip of my mimosa. "Nothing like that. Everything was going so well, and then he just ghosted me." Tears of anger welled up in my eyes.

Alex laughed nervously. "Maybe he's really busy, you know. Billy told me his divorce is almost final. That seems like a good reason for keeping head low, at least to me."

"He should have told me that, then," I said angrily. "It's been a week since I heard from him, and he's been keeping his cell phone turned off!"

Alex furrowed her brow. She reached into the box of cupcakes and bit into one, wiping pink icing from her upper lip.

"I don't know," she said. "Maybe he thought things were getting too fast, too soon? That's how I felt when I first met Billy," she offered.

I glared at her. "Then he's a coward, and he should've told me himself." I sniffed angrily as tears welled up in my eyes. "I'm just so sick of this!" I snapped, getting to my feet and looking around.

"What? Elisabeth, it'll be okay," Alex said. "Whatever is going on with him, I'm sure it'll work out, okay?"

I glared at her. "Yeah, right," I snapped. "I just wanna get the fuck out of Savannah and never come back!"

Alex bit her lip. I watched as she dialed a number on her phone and set the device down on my table. Soon, a feminine voice chirped through my kitchen.

"Hello, thank you for calling Rocker and Powell, Attorneys at Law! How may I help you?"

"Hi, this is Alex – could I please talk with my husband?"

"Oh my gosh, Mrs. Lessner! I didn't recognize your voice! Of course, I'll put you right through."

Seconds later, Billy's voice boomed over the speaker.

"Hey, baby, what's up?" Billy drawled. "You doin' okay?"

"Yes," Alex said. She frowned. "I was just wondering if you heard from Damien."

"Edwards?"

"Yeah," Alex said. "Have you?"

Billy cleared his throat. "Yeah," he said. "He called in a few days ago, wanted to check on how fast things were movin' along. What's wrong?"

"Nothing," Alex said. She glanced at me. "Did he say anything about Elisabeth?"

"Well, shoot," Billy said. "Yeah, he did, actually."

"What?" Alex asked. My heart was racing as I leaned closer to the phone.

Billy sighed. "It's real fucked up," he said. "Said that his ex, Candace, was trying to blackmail him with some pictures of he and Elisabeth, screwin' in the back of his car. He was real broken up, honey, but he panicked and figured he oughta cut things off, so the court would still find him respectable."

My heart sank and Alex looked at me sympathetically.

"Okay," she said. "Thanks, hon. I love you, I'll see you later."

"Am I on speaker phone? I can't barely hear you, hon."

"Don't worry about it," Alex called loudly. "See you when you get home."

She hung up and turned to me, biting her lip.

"I'm sorry," Alex said. "I…I had no idea. I would've told you if I knew sooner, I swear."

My shoulders sank and I buried my face in my hands. "I know," I mumbled.

The truth was, as much as I still wanted to be angry with Damien, I suddenly understood. I understood that his girls were more important, that his family had to come first.

But I couldn't deny that my heart had broken in two. This was somehow worse than Damien deciding he no longer wanted anything to do with me. His hands were tied.

And now, I was never going to see him again.

9

***

I tried hard to distract myself after Billy had given me the terrible news about Damien. I was good. I didn't call, try to text, or even bother his office again. But I couldn't stop thinking about him. Every time I closed my eyes, Damien's handsome face flashed in front of my mind.

I knew I was going to have to work a lot harder if I really wanted to get over him.

I'd been thinking about leaving Savannah, and honestly this seemed like as good of a time as any. I packed up a few of the vases and pots that I'd made recently, including a teapot shaped like a dragon, and drove downtown to the shop where I often taught classes.

My friend, Nadine, was behind the counter. When she saw me struggling with a heavy box, she ran over and took it from my hands.

"Wow, Elisabeth," Nadine said. "This is a ton of work. And it's all beautiful," she added. "Especially this."

"Thanks." I sighed. "Thinking about moving and I was wondering if we could sell any of these."

Nadine carefully lifted the pieces out, cradling each one in her hand. "We can sell all of these," she said. "And I love this teapot!"

"Thanks," I said. "It did turn out well."

Nadine narrowed her eyes. "Yeah," she said. She glanced over the red-glazed pot and nodded. "I'll put this stuff in the inventory as soon as I have some free time. Why not hang out for a while, I should be able to get to everything soon."

I nodded. As Nadine dealt with customers and her new increase in stock, I wandered around, looking carefully at the different displays. Savannah was home to a lot of talented artists, but after living here for years, I knew them all. And honestly, I was starting to crave a new adventure. I'd been happy here, but it was time for something different. I wondered if maybe I wouldn't be better suited to a bigger city, like Boston, or Portland.

It seemed to take hours for Nadine to catch up on her back log. I turned my attention to the workshop in the back – it was filthy and streaked with dried clay. Rolling my eyes, I pulled on an apron and started to clean.

"You don't have to do that."

I looked up to see an unfamiliar guy, walking towards me and smiling. He was cute, in the artsy kind of way – long blonde hair pulled into a loose knot at the back of his neck, tanned skin. He was wearing a gauzy shirt that reminded me of something Indian peasants would have worn.

"I know," I said. I jerked my head towards Nadine. "I'm a friend of hers, we went to art school together. She's going to sell some of my work."

The guy grinned. He reached out his hand for a shake. After a second, I accepted.

"I'm Bear," he said.

I rolled my eyes. "Of course you are. I'm Elisabeth," I added. "You new in town?"

Bear shrugged. "I come and I go," he said. "But I've never seen you here before." He grinned wolfishly. "How about showing me around?"

I shook my head. "No, thanks."

Bear laughed. "Oh, I get it," he said. "You've already got someone."

"Not really," I said. "I just don't feel like dating at the moment."

Bear leaned in close and raised an eyebrow. "Hey, if you're a dyke, it's cool with me," he said. "You don't have to lie about it."

I narrowed my eyes. "Excuse me?"

Bear held up his hands and grinned, clearly pleased with his cocky remark. "I get it," he said. "Nadine's a real babe. I've been trying to fuck her for years. I wouldn't blame you if you wanted a shot."

I glared at him. "Fuck off, you disrespectful asshole," I said. I pushed past Bear and walked to the front of the store where Nadine stood, chatting with a customer.

"You okay?" Nadine glanced up with concern. "Your aura seems angry, Elisabeth."

"That guy is such an asshole," I hissed, pointing to Bear and glaring. "He actually just called me a lesbian because I said I didn't want to go out with him."

Nadine rolled her eyes and tossed her hair. "Typical wounded man-ego," she said, snorting. "Don't pay attention to him."

I took a deep breath. "Yeah," I said. "Better not let myself get so worked up."

It was funny. When Damien and I had first met, I'd assumed he was the same way. Rude, arrogant – the kind of man who thinks he's always to get his way with a woman around. But once I'd gotten to know him, I'd realized just how very wrong I was.

Thinking of him now made me want to break down in tears.

"So," Nadine said. "I think we can start the pricing for these around four hundred, what do you think?"

I shrugged. "I don't care," I said. "They're out of my house, that's kind of the only goal at hand."

Nadine narrowed her eyes. "You seem depressed," she said. "I'm having a get-together later, you want to come?" Reaching across the counter, she handed me a stack of polaroids. "These are from my last party. See how much fun?"

I frowned as I flipped through the pictures. Nadine's Bohemian-style living room was littered with artsy people, all posing in long caftans and flower crowns. Everyone seemed to be having fun – there was a large tub of sangria on the table – and all the faces were smiling and happy. I recognized most of the people, too: they were all people who had done business with Nadine over the years. Some of them were even people I'd taught before.

When I got to a picture of a beautiful woman leaning over a mirror covered with small lines of white powder. She had caramel-colored hair, twisted back in a chignon, and she was smiling with lips that looked too full to be natural.

I narrowed my eyes. She looked familiar, somehow, even though I was sure I'd never met her before. At least, I *thought* I was sure.

"Who is that?" I asked nonchalantly, sticking the photo under Nadine's nose.

She rolled her eyes. "Oh, gods," she said. "That's Candace." Nadine wrinkled her nose. "She was such a bitch, but she came as this one guy's date – you remember James? The guy who sculpts out of flatware?"

"What did you say?"

Nadine gave me a suspicious look. "I said, that's Candace," she said slowly. "She's not really in my circle of friends. Why? Do you know her?"

I bit my lip. Savannah wasn't that small of a city, but suddenly I felt like I'd just stumbled upon the proverbial pot of gold.

"I think so," I said slowly. "At least, I've heard of her. Is she married?"

"She's getting divorced," Nadine replied. "It was like, all she talked about. For hours, she couldn't shut up about how much her life sucks now because her husband found out she was cheating."

Squinting, I held the photo up to my face. I breathed a sigh of relief when I noticed the film was dated – from just two weeks ago.

"Do you mind if I keep this?"

Nadine laughed nervously. "You'd better not go around telling anyone I had blow in my house," she said anxiously. "I mean, please don't do that."

I shook my head. "Don't worry," I said. "Nothing like that."

Nadine looked relieved. "Then sure, I don't mind if you take it," she said. "Go ahead, hell, take them all if you like."

I smiled as I slipped the photo into my purse. "Oh, don't worry," I said. "I've got exactly what I need."

As I left the pottery studio, I couldn't help but grin. While I knew next to nothing about the law, I had a feeling that this compromising photo of Candace would certainly help Billy in court...especially if she knew nothing about it before it was shown.

I drove to Rocker & Powell, Attorneys at Law with my foot on the gas the whole time. Butterflies were swarming around in my stomach – I wondered if somehow, this would help Damien. I realized that no matter what, even if we were never together again, that was all I wanted for him. Candace was obviously a terrible mother to Arabella and Annaliese, and Damien was hoping for full custody.

I pulled into the parking lot, desperately relieved when I saw that Damien's car was nowhere in sight. Breathlessly, I grabbed my purse and ran into the office, glancing around and making a beeline for Billy's door.

"Excuse me," a girl said, narrowing her eyes. "Do you have an appointment? Can I help you?"

I grinned smugly. Just as I was about to answer her, Billy's door swung open and he sauntered out, clad in a shirt rolled to the elbows and a smart pair of dark trousers. When he saw me, he narrowed his eyes.

"Elisabeth? What are you doing here?"

I licked my lips and pulled the photo out of my purse, smiling triumphantly. "I thought this could help you," I said, raising an eyebrow as Billy pulled the photo close and examined it.

"Where did you get this?" Billy looked up at me and I could tell his mind was spinning.

"Does it matter?"

Billy grinned. "No," he said. "It really doesn't."

10

***

I wouldn't have admitted to anyone other than Alex, but when Damien didn't automatically rush over after I gave Billy that photo, it stung.

Just a little bit, though.

I knew – rationally, at least – that Damien would need some time. I just hoped that he'd want to come back to me.

I tried to stay busy. At Nadine's request, I taught three days in a row down at her pottery shop. I wasn't sure whether I still felt like moving away from Savannah, but I did some research on Portland and Harper's Ferry. Maybe it was time for a change. And if things didn't wind up working out with Damien, well, I'd gotten a taste of love and excitement. Alex suggested I make a dating profile online, but the suggestion just made me wrinkle my nose.

"So you're *not* over him, then," Alex said. She raised her eyebrows and sipped from her mug of tea without breaking eye contact.

I sighed. "I don't know what I am," I said. I bit my lip. "For the longest time, I was just so angry with Richard for ruining my life. And now..."

"And now?"

I flushed hotly. "And now I'm starting to realize that Richard and I were never right for each other." I wrinkled my nose. "It sounds weird, but I'm almost grateful."

"For what?" Alex laughed. "That's an odd way to put it."

"I know," I said quickly. "But I'm almost happy that we divorced, you know?" I felt a sharp pang in my chest and I took a long swallow of tea. "Like, because otherwise, I never would've met Damien. I wouldn't have known what true love feels like."

Alex frowned and nodded. "Yeah," she said quietly. "I understand that."

I sighed. "I just...I really miss him, Alex." I licked my lips. "I never felt the way I felt when I was around Damien. Never before, not in my whole life."

"If it's meant to happen, it will," Alex said. "Things work out. Remember – if everything isn't okay, then it's not the end."

I nodded. "I think you're more optimistic than I am," I said quietly. I sighed, blowing wisps of brown hair away from my face. "Maybe I should just feel lucky that I got the chance to fall in love at all."

Alex nodded. "If you want my opinion, I know Damien really liked you, Elisabeth. I'm wondering if he's not waiting for everything to be finalized before he contacts you again."

I frowned. "That could take over a year," I said. "I might be gone by then."

Alex reached out and put her hand on my shoulder. "Well, would you consider sticking around if it meant making things work with Damien?"

My stomach twisted and I swallowed. "I don't know," I said honestly. "I don't really want to talk about this anymore."

Alex nodded. "Sorry," she said. "Hey, wanna come over for dinner later? Billy's working late, so I'm just making yumasetta."

I shrugged. “I don’t know,” I said. “I’m not really hungry.”

Alex frowned. “Look, I know this is hard,” she said. “But you have to stay strong, okay?”

I nodded, then got up from my seat and stretched. “I think I’m going to go for a walk,” I said. “You want any more tea?”

Alex shook her head. I could tell by the painful look of her face that she wanted to say more, but honestly, I just wanted to be alone. I knew that Alex was trying to help – she was my best friend, after all – but somehow, talking about it just made me feel worse. And it was hard for me not to feel bitter. After all, Alex had gotten her happy ending. She’d gotten to marry the love of her life.

But I’d never been a lucky person. And I saw absolutely no reason for things to change now.

“Hey, promise you’ll tell me if you really think about leaving here,” Alex said. “I don’t want to wake up one morning and find that my best friend has left town.” She said it lightly, but her words branded me with guilt all the same. Knowing me, that was exactly what I’d do – leave in the middle of the night, without telling anyone.

"I will," I said. I glanced around at all of the art covering my walls. "Besides, it would take me a few days to pack up all of this junk."

"Elisabeth..."

"I'm fine," I snapped quickly, getting to my feet and forcing a smile. "I'll think about dinner, okay?"

Alex nodded, looking only slightly relieved. "Okay," she said. "You don't have to call, just show up, okay?"

I nodded. "See you later."

I watched as Alex slowly walked to my door. I knew she was hoping I'd invite her to stay longer, but I couldn't handle pretending to be fine for another second. As we hugged, I made a mental vow to keep myself as calm as possible.

But that was short lived. As soon as Alex had gone, I raced into my living room and grabbed my laptop. I couldn't stop myself from searching Damien's name, and rereading that piece about his success over and over. Resentment bubbled up in my throat when I saw Candace's picture. In this piece, she looked every inch the perfect wife. There was no trace of the smug, smiling person over a tray of coke.

When I heard the sound of someone knocking at my door, I rolled my eyes. *Leave it alone, Alex*, I thought angrily. *I told you, I want to be left alone.*

My eyes were narrowed into angry slits as I stalked down the hall and yanked open the door. Just as I was about to spew a litany of curses, I realized that Damien was standing there. His dark eyes were wide and for once, he actually looked nervous.

"Hi," Damien said quietly. "Can I come in?"

A rush of emotions flew through my body and I bit my lip. "Yeah," I said softly. "Sure."

I stepped back to let Damien inside. As always, the tension between us felt thick and crackling, almost like the air was full of static electricity.

It worked, I thought slowly as I followed Damien into the living room. *I can't believe it worked!* I felt my bad mood slipping away like a rolling cloud. I knew that I should at least be a little angry – after all, he still could've reached out instead of ghosting me. And I knew that it was pathetic that I was so ready to take him back.

But I didn't care. I'd truly fallen in love.

"It's nice to see you," I said, sinking down on the couch.

Damien nodded stiffly. "Yeah," he said. "Look, Elisabeth – I'm really sorry. I should've called you."

"Yeah," I said. I sighed. "But it's okay, I understand. Billy told me everything."

Damien nodded.

"I'm just glad it worked," I said, breathing in with satisfaction. My lips curled into a smile. "I was really thinking I'd never see you again."

Damien narrowed his eyes. "What?"

"The photo," I said. "You know, the one I took to Billy. It must've worked!"

"What photo?" Damien frowned. "Elisabeth, I'm sorry – I don't know what you're talking about."

"Come on," I said. I laughed nervously – the sound echoed off the walls. Suddenly, anxiety trickled down into my stomach. *What if he's not here because he wants to stay together*, I thought as my anxiety snowballed into an avalanche of panic. *What if he only came became he has the decency to break up with me in person?!*

"I really don't," Damien said. "Don't play coy," he said. "What are you talking about?"

"I can't believe you don't know," I said slowly.

"Elisabeth, out with it!" Damien's eyes flashed with a hot intensity. "Don't play games with me."

"I went down to the pottery studio the other day," I said quickly. "And Nadine – she's the owner, we're friends, we went to art school together – was trying to get me to come to some party at her place. She showed me pictures from an older party, a couple of weeks back, and there was a picture of Candace."

"Doing what?" Damien's voice came out as a growl.

"She was sitting in front of a mirror full of blow," I said. "And she was holding a straw."

Damien's face went white. "This was just a few weeks ago?" He growled in anger.

"Yeah," I said nervously. Damien's rage was so palpable that I could feel it sinking into my skin.

"She still has joint custody," Damien growled angrily.

"I know," I said quickly. "As soon as I saw the picture, I took it straight to Billy. I thought it could help you," I said softly. "I was only trying to help."

Damien's face relaxed and he nodded. "I know," he said.

"But why didn't Billy tell you?"

A muscle twitched in Damien's clenched jaw. "I don't know," he said. "I'm guessing it's because he wanted to take some time and try to think about how this would affect the case. I'm not a lawyer, but obviously I'm hoping this doesn't go to court."

I nodded. Somehow, that just made me feel worse. *He's going to dump me*, I realized. *And he's going to do it right now, and I don't fucking know how I'm going to manage to stay calm and not cry. Fuck!* A lump swelled in my throat and my eyes filled with tears.

Damien reached out and put his hand on my shoulder. I knew I should resist – push him away, do anything so I could steel myself against the barrage of words that was sure to make my world come crashing down. I wished I'd taken Alex up on her offer for dinner. I wished I hadn't let her leave. I wished—

"Elisabeth? What's wrong?"

"Why are you here?" I asked quietly. "If you didn't know about the photo, why did you bother coming over here? To break up with me," I muttered bitterly. "You could've just called."

"No," Damien said.

I sighed impatiently. "Just get it over with," I said hotly.

Before I could do anything else, Damien pulled me close and kissed me. I gasped as he pressed his lips to mine, passionately kissing me. He took my face in his hands and pulled me close, erasing the gap between us. As his tongue slid into my mouth, I closed my eyes and moaned softly. Impatient arousal swirled through my belly. Even though I knew I should push him away, I couldn't help myself. I was finally with Damien again, and that was all that mattered.

When he pulled away, Damien looked flushed and breathless. "No," he said. "I'm not here because I want to break up with you." He shook his head. "I'm here because I don't care what Candace has against me. I don't give a fuck. You're what matters to me, Elisabeth. I've fallen in love with you and I can't let you go."

I gasped.

Damien raised an eyebrow. "Not what you were expecting, I bet," he said bitterly. "I feel like such an asshole for not being in touch sooner, Elisabeth. The truth is…when Candace told me she had those photos, I felt like a coward. I felt like I was living some kind of double life – pretending to be a good parent to my girls while seeing you on the side. And it made me feel ashamed," he added hotly. "I've never been comfortable with myself, and I couldn't stomach the possibility of losing my children."

"I hope you don't," I said quietly.

Damien shook his head impatiently. "I don't think I will," he said. "I've got the best lawyer in town, and I'm more than willing to pay Candace whatever she wants." He rolled his eyes. "Money is the only thing she cares about anyway," he added. "She doesn't want the responsibility of being a parent."

I blinked. "So...you're okay with dating me, even if you get full custody of the girls?"

Damien nodded. "That's the best case scenario," he said hotly. "I can't stay away from you, Elisabeth. You've become so important to me."

I blushed hotly. "I love you," I said softly.

Damien pulled me into a close embrace. My heart fluttered as he kissed my temples.

"I love you," Damien said tenderly.

Before I could reply, Damien slipped his arm under my legs and scooped me up. Our lips met as he carried me down the hall and into my bedroom. I was barely aware of my body dropping to the bed. Damien crawled on top of me and kissed me passionately, pressing me into the mattress with his lean bulk. I moaned softly and wrapped my arms around his neck as he slipped his hands under my shirt and tugged it away from my body.

"You're so beautiful," Damien whispered as he stroked his hands down my body. I shivered at the warmth of his touch – it was so incredible, so perfect that I could barely breathe. I'd never felt an intense love like the one I felt with Damien – I'd never even thought it was possible.

Damien flipped his head and the ends of his dark, silky hair brushed my skin. I put my hands on his strong shoulders and pulled him closer, kissing him until my lips were raw and my jaw ached. Damien chuckled. He crossed his arms over his chest and pulled his shirt off, his lean muscles gleaming in the low light of my bedroom. When our skin collided, a happiness burst in my body. My lower belly was tight with arousal and my clit was throbbing, already aching for Damien's touch. As Damien reached behind my body and unfastened my bra, I arched my back. His lips left a scorching trail on my skin as he kissed my neck, nipping gently at the delicate skin until I cried out.

When Damien started to rub and roll my stiff nipples between his fingers, I thought I would die of pleasure. I cried out and gasped as delicious sensations raced through my body, setting every cell on a fire with passion. I tangled my hands in his silky hair and pulled him close as I pressed my lips to his. Damien growled with passion. He pushed my hands away, then flipped me onto my belly before I could resist. I blushed hotly as Damien reached under my body and fumbled with the snap of my jeans. He tugged them down my hips and I moaned as he slid a warm hand between my thighs. Damien gently rubbed my clit through the soaked crotch of my panties. Instinctively, I spread my legs as far as I could, burying my face in the pillows and moaning as his touch became more intense.

Hot lust crawled through my belly and I moaned again, gasping as Damien slipped a finger inside my panties and inside of me. He wriggled his fingers, pushing his hand hard against my clit until I cried out with pleasure.

Damien chuckled. "I love you this way," he growled. "Begging and panting and moaning for more."

My blush deepened to a crimson red and I let out a strangled cry of pleasure. Damien ripped my panties away from my body. I felt his weight shift on the bed as he crawled between my legs.

"Do you trust me," Damien growled.

"Yes," I whispered.

The tension was insanely high. I closed my eyes, listening to every single sound in the room. There was a *whish* as Damien pulled his belt from his hands. I jumped at the next sound – a light *smack!* that made me think he'd doubled his belt and smacked his palm.

When the first light smack of the belt landed on my bare ass, I yelped. It hurt, but it also felt better than I could have ever imagined. The pain somehow mingled with my pleasure, making it more intense. I cried out and arched my back, sticking my ass in the air, wanting more.

I could practically hear Damien smirking.

"You're a bad girl," Damien purred. Seconds later, the belt landed again on my ass and I moaned. Wriggling on the bed, I spread my legs as far as I could. Damien chuckled. When I felt his thumb probing my clit, I moaned loudly. Soon, the belt was gently spanking me in time with Damien's rhythmic touch. I could feel my orgasm building powerfully in my lower belly as I clenched handfuls of the duvet.

"I can't wait anymore," Damien growled. I lay waiting, every inch of my body wanting more, as the sound of Damien pulling his jeans off filled the room. Soon he was back between my thighs, grabbing fistfuls of my ass and making me cry out with pleasure. His hard cock probed at the entrance to my wet pussy, and I moaned, wriggling my hips in the air as I waited for him to take me.

Damien grabbed my hip and rolled me over onto my back. I gasped as he spread my legs, crawled between my thighs, and plunged deep inside of me. The force of his cock slamming into my body made me scream with pleasure. Damien tangled his fingers with mine and held my arms over my head. Our bodies were stretched and taut, and I closed my eyes and arched my back as he covered my face and neck with kisses.

I wrapped both of my legs around Damien's waist, holding him deep inside of me and wriggling my body against his. He purred and growled, shoving his hips against my sweaty abdomen. When I felt his pubic bone graze against my clit, I knew I wouldn't be able to hold back for much longer. My ass was deliciously sore and every time I moved, a shock of pain mingled with pleasure shot through my body. Damien nipped at my lower lip and slipped his tongue inside my mouth, making me moan. As I sucked on his lips, Damien released my hands and began massaging my breasts with his fingers. The firm touch was all I needed, and soon I was bucking and gasping as my orgasm tore through my body.

"God," Damien groaned. "Oh, god, Elisabeth, I can't wait anymore!"

I shrieked with pleasure as Damien buried his face in my neck. My body was filled with a haze of post-orgasmic bliss and I could barely keep from purring like a happy kitten as Damien's cock plunged inside of me, deeper than ever, again and again. When his own orgasm hit, his body twitched and strained against mine. His cock throbbed inside of me and I moaned, twisting my body close to his and holding him as tightly as I could.

When he was finished, Damien collapsed against me. His sweaty limbs entwined with mine and we both sighed happily as he closed his eyes and rested his elegant face against my chest.

"I love you," Damien said quietly. "Thank you, Elisabeth. I wasn't sure if you'd give me another chance."

I licked my dry lips and stroked his sweaty hair. "I love you," I said. "I...I don't think I'd be able to stay away from you, Damien."

Damien's lips curled into a hint of a smile.

"I was thinking about if I should leave Savannah," I said softly. "But now...I don't want to go."

"If you could go anywhere, where would you?"

I twined my fingers with Damien's and squeezed. "Anywhere," I said. "As long as it's with you, I don't care."

Damien grinned. He kissed the side of my breast. "Good answer," he said. "But I couldn't blame you for wanting to leave."

"Your business, though," I said. I rolled onto my side and curled close to Damien. "You couldn't leave that, could you?"

Damien shrugged. "I could work from anywhere," he said. "But it depends on how this whole custody thing shakes out. Truth be told, I want my girls far away from Candace. But I'll have to wait and see."

I hugged him close. "We'll just have to wait together," I said, brushing his hair away from his brow.

Damien leaned close and kissed me. "I'm fine with that," he said softly.

I blushed. "Me, too," I whispered. "Me, too."

11

***

One Year Later

"Daddy! I can't find my other shoe!" Arabella raced into the bedroom, her dark hair trailing a flag behind her.

Damien shook his head. "Well, wear another pair," he said crossly. "We're going to be late if you can't hurry."

"I'll help you look," I said quickly, taking Arabella by the hand and leading her out of the bedroom.

"Daddy's in a bad mood," Arabella whispered as we walked down the hall and into the room she shared with Annaliese. "He never yells."

"He didn't yell," I said. "But yeah, he's not feeling so well."

Arabella pouted.

"Don't worry," I said quickly. "Daddy still loves you both, very much. He's not upset because of you, I promise."

Arabella nodded. I had to hide a smile – she was easily the most intense six-year-old that I'd ever met.

Annaliese was sitting on the bed, her dress half-buttoned. She was swinging her legs back and forth and there was a coloring book on her lap. She barely looked up when I walked in with her sister in tow.

"Annaliese, we're leaving soon," I said. "Are you ready?"

Annaliese shrugged. "I don't care," she said.

I rolled my eyes. "Honey, come on – this isn't going to take long. And didn't your dad say that we could all go out to dinner later?"

Annaliese shrugged again. Her lips were pouting and her cheeks were puffed out.

"What if I help you pick another outfit," I said. "Wouldn't that be fun?"

Annaliese shrugged her tiny shoulders. "I don't know," she said. "I don't care. I don't want to go."

Frowning, I sat down on the floor and crossed my legs. "What's wrong?" I asked gently. "Is there something really bothering you, honey?"

Annaliese sniffled. She climbed off the bed and came closer to me, resting her head against my thigh.

"I don't want to go," she said. She wiped her nose on the back of her hand. "I don't want the man to make us go live with Mommy."

"Oh, honey." I wrapped my arms around Annaliese and pulled her into a hug. "Is that what you're afraid of?"

Annaliese nodded. "I don't want to live with her," she said. "I like being here with you and Daddy."

To my surprise, tears welled up in my eyes. I sniffled, tilting my head to the ceiling so neither girl would see me cry.

"I don't think you have anything to worry about," I said quickly. "Besides, we're not going to court. We're just going to Mr. Billy's office – you remember him, right?"

Annaliese nodded. She sighed, blowing her dark bangs into the air. "I don't want to go," she repeated stubbornly.

"Girls! We need to get a move on!" Damien's voice thundered down the hall and into the room.

"Come on," I cajoled Annaliese. "This isn't going to be bad at all, I promise. We're not even going to be in the room, we'll be outside doing our own thing."

"I know," Annaliese said crossly. "That's why I'm so upset. I want to talk to the lawyer. I want to tell him that I don't want to live with Mommy."

I sighed. "I know. But you're just going to have to trust your father, okay? He loves both of you girls more than anything, and I promise, he knows exactly how you feel."

Annaliese and Arabella exchanged a nervous glance. Finally, Annaliese got to her feet and went to the closet. She changed into a different dress, then tied a ribbon in her hair.

"I'm ready," she said.

"Arabella, do you have a pair of shoes?"

Arabella nodded. I offered both girls my hands. "Let's go," I said. "We don't want to make him late."

After a long, arduous process, the day had finally come. Damien was meeting with Billy, Candace, and Candace's lawyer to settle their case out of court. Damien had initially been optimistic, but in the last couple of days, I'd noticed that he was anxious and frightened of the outcome. Billy had shown the photo of Candace and the cocaine to her lawyer, and while he was confident of a good outcome, Damien was still nervous that things wouldn't go well.

Damien was pacing back and forth in the kitchen. When he saw me bring in the girls, he nodded.

"Come on," Damien said. "We've got to really hurry."

I helped Arabella and Annaliese into the car, then sat nervously as Damien drove into Savannah. When we got to Rocker and Powell, Attorneys at Law, Damien gave me a nervous kiss on the forehead. He pulled both girls into a tight hug.

"We'll just be over here," I said, nodding towards the small public park across the street from Billy's law offices. "I'll be thinking good thoughts."

Damien nodded. "I know," he said. "Thank you for coming and taking care of the girls today. I know this can't be fun for you."

"They're nervous, too," I said. "They're afraid they'll have to live with Candace."

Damien's mouth hardened into a scowl. "Not if I have anything to say about it," he growled. He gave me one last kiss, then walked inside like a man going to his death.

"Come on, girls," I said. "Let's go play on the swings while we wait for your dad, okay?"

Arabella and Annaliese nodded. I took each of their hands, then led them across the street and into the park.

I'd only been living with Damien for about six months. We'd wanted to move in right away, but we'd both been concerned for the welfare of the girls. And while there had initially been a little tension, I felt like I'd finally found a good balance of being a "cool older friend" and "occasional stepmother." Being around Arabella and Annaliese really made me think about kids in a different way. I still loved Alex's son, Jacob, but he was younger than the twins. It was shocking to me that first-graders could be so smart and articulate. I didn't remember anything like that from when I was a kid – everything had been messy playground fights and sweaty palms.

The minutes seemed to tick by more slowly than usual as I sat in the park, watching Annaliese and Arabella play on the swings. They were chattering animatedly – at least *they* had finally relaxed. I knew that the divorce finalization shouldn't take that long, but I also knew that Candace was going to try every trick in the book to get as much as she possibly could from Damien. It really made me angry to think of a woman like her taking advantage of the man I loved.

But if that was the price I had to pay for being with Damien, I would've paid it a thousand times over.

Nearly two hours passed before the door opened and I watched Damien and Billy walk outside. They shook hands, then Damien started across the street. His expression was blank and neutral. The girls hadn't noticed – they were still swinging back and forth, kicking their little legs high in the air.

I practically ran towards Damien. When he saw me, he smiled.

"What happened?" I asked breathlessly. "How did things go?"

Damien's smile grew an inch wider. "Very well," he said. "I got it."

"You did?" Tears welled up in my eyes and I threw my arms around Damien's neck, pulling him close. "I'm so happy! I can't believe it!"

Damien grinned. He kissed me chastely, then nodded. "Yeah," he said. "Turns out Billy showed that picture of Candace to her lawyer, and everything was pretty much settled from there. She was actually the one who pushed for this to settle out of court – she knew that a judge would really dress her down if she tried for anything."

I reached for Damien's hand and squeezed. "The girls are going to be so happy," I said. I glanced over my shoulder. Arabella and Annaliese were still playing, oblivious to the return of their father.

Damien nodded. "I couldn't be happier," he

said. "This is really incredible. I can't believe it's finally over." He kissed me again and wrapped an arm around my shoulders. "I'd really like to go out to dinner with you."

"Well, yeah," I said. "You promised us all lunch, after all."

Damien shook his head. "Lunch with the girls, then dinner with you. Alone," he added, raising an eyebrow and smirking at me. "To celebrate."

"Sounds good," I said. I grinned.

"I have a sitter lined up," Damien said. "I sorta had a feeling things would turn out like this, I just didn't want to count my chickens before they hatched."

"Yeah," I said. "I get that."

"Besides, we'll have something extra special to celebrate, just the two of us," Damien said. He raised an eyebrow at me.

I cocked my head to the side. "What are you talking about?"

Damien dropped gracefully down to one knee and I gasped. When he pulled a small velvet box from the pocket of his coat, I covered my mouth with both hands.

"Marry me, Elisabeth," Damien said. "I love you, and I can't imagine life without you."

He opened the box and I shrieked. Inside was a platinum ring with a large center stone – a diamond – surrounded by sapphires.

"It's beautiful," I said softly.

There were two smaller rings in the box, too – each a small infinity band with diamonds.

"Yes," I said. "Yes, yes, yes!"

Damien slipped the three rings onto my finger. "The smaller ones are from the girls," he said. "When we decided that we wanted you to join the family, they wanted to pick a ring for you, too."

Tears were streaming down my face as I wrapped my arms around Damien's shoulders and buried my face in his neck.

"Did she say yes?"

"Yeah, Daddy! Did she say yes?"

Arabella and Annaliese giggled as they danced around us, chanting and cheering. I knew I should hug them, too, and thank them for the rings – but I couldn't take my mind off Damien.

As we stood together in the park, a new family risen from the ashes, I knew that no matter what the future held, it would be perfect. If I had Damien and the girls, I'd always be happy.

Join Our Exclusive E-Mail List!

***

Click HERE or copy and paste http://bit.ly/2swDl1l into your web browser to join. You will get another FREE eBook, Easton's Crime: A Second Chance, written by my close friend Audrey North!

Printed in Great Britain
by Amazon